Trevor Hoyle has been w
years, producing mainly novels and short stories but also tele-
vision drama scripts and reviews. He also lectures to colleges
and writing groups and has worked as a writer-in-residence.
His novels include *The Relatively Constant Copywriter*, *Rule of
Night*, *The 'Q' Series*, a science fiction trilogy, *The Man Who
Travelled on Motorways* and *K.I.D.S.* (Sphere 1987). He is a past
winner of the 'Transatlantic Review' short story competition
(British section) and has been on the judging panel for the
Constable Novel Competition. Trevor Hoyle was born in
Lancashire where he still lives.

Also by Trevor Hoyle in Sphere Books:

K.I.D.S.

VAIL

Trevor Hoyle

ABACUS

SPHERE BOOKS

Published by the Penguin Group
27 Wrights Lane, London W8 5TZ, England
Viking Penguin Inc., 40 West 23rd Street, New York, New York 10010, USA
Penguin Books Australia Ltd, Ringwood, Victoria, Australia
Penguin Books Canada Ltd, 2801 John Street, Markham, Ontario, Canada L3R 1B4
Penguin Books (NZ) Ltd, 182–190 Wairau Road, Auckland 10, New Zealand

Penguin Books Ltd, Registered Offices: Harmondsworth, Middlesex, England

First published in Great Britain by John Calder (Publishers Limited) 1984
Published in Abacus by Sphere Books Limited 1989
1 3 5 7 9 10 8 6 4 2

Made and printed in Great Britain by
Richard Clay Ltd, Bungay, Suffolk

To John Calder

A CHRISTIAN PRAYER

Lord, make me an instrument of Thy peace:
Where there is hatred, let me sow love;
Where there is injury, pardon;
Where there is discord, union;
Where there is doubt, faith;
Where there is despair, hope;
Where there is darkness, light;
Where there is sadness, joy.
O Divine Master, grant that I may not so much seek
To be consoled as to console;
To be understood, as to understand;
To be loved, as to love;
For it is in giving that we receive,
It is in pardoning, that we are pardoned;
And it is in dying that we are born
To eternal life.

St Francis of Assisi

[1]

Vail had been in London less than a fortnight and had been accosted four times by the police. Each time he had given them a different name, address and occupation. Either they were incompetent or the national computer wasn't functioning properly, or his luck was just too good to be true. Then again, maybe they really couldn't care less: he was a scrounger, a layabout, a fringer,—no real threat to society except perhaps for a spot of petty larceny and the odd rape here and there. Why waste a cell on a useless *swmbwl* such as him?

If they locked up all the useless *swmbwls* they could find there wouldn't be room for the Krays and Kagans of this world.

He could remember the moment of decision exactly. It occurred while he was standing on the pavement outside an electrical retailer's at twenty minutes past ten one night watching twenty-two television screens showing the same identical face. A woman in a beige hip-length coat walked by and laughed in her throat at his expression. Vail didn't hear,—or if he did paid no attention: his gaze was fixed, rabid. The idea seemed very simple and obvious, and he wondered why he hadn't thought of it before.

[*The reason was that until this minute he'd never contemplated killing anyone. Most people don't, as an act of retribution, much less as the solution to their problems.*]

Vail is now firmly committed to this course of action, and while he hasn't formulated the means of carrying it out, and knows it will be difficult (some might say impossible), he isn't too much concerned. He has a naïve faith in the inevitability of the evolutionary imperative: nature fills an available niche, abhors a vacuum, etc. It had to be and therefore would come to pass.

Sooner or later an Opportunity will present itself.

He goes home to his cardboard box under the viaduct off Southwark Park Road and beds down for the night. It is balmy August. Vail composes himself for sleep, and drifts away, despite the frostbite nibbling hotly at feet and hands.

[2]

His belly full of Salvation Army pea soup, Vail sets off on another aimless ramble of the capital. Tourists everywhere. It is cloudy and heavy, a torpid sort of day. Smells come from the drains and mingle with the dense blue vapour of the traffic. Near a sandbagged sterile enclosure in the vicinity of Piccadilly Circus he overhears a conversation:

"And I'm telling you, Freesia-Belle,—the South Bank is *this* way!"

"All righty, I believe you. But can't we get the toob? I'm so *hot*,"—suffering complaint.

"I thought you wanted to see the ass-hole of the universe? You don't see it underground. Just diarrhoea and vomit!"

"Let me imagine."

"Listen: imagine in your own time on your own money. I didn't sell four hundred twenty-eight Datsuns because I love the Japanese junk!"

"I'm too hot, honey. Can't we take a cab?"

"And get lice? Are you serious?"

"Well at least can't we . . ."

"What, for chrissakes!"

Whispers.

"What?"

"That man."

"Huh?"

"He's listening to us."

6

"Can we do anything for you, mister?"

"Now, honey, don't be . . ."

"I don't give a goddamn! *Well?*"

Vail stares for a moment, blinks, moves on.

"He wasn't begging, Spud."

"Just let him try! I've stepped on better looking roaches . . ."

Vail presses his face to the diamond mesh of the perimeter fence around Hyde Park and looks at the dewy sprinklered grass. The greenness makes him swoon. He can see Enid Blyton in the shimmering haze perambulating to her dressmaker's. She moves incorporeally along the neat gravelled paths to the sound of chimes calling the hour. England trails in her wake like a dozy playful poodle. Her face is smooth, padded, rosy, bountiful. In her eyes are hatpins.

[3]

A man touches Vail's shoulder.

"I know you, don't I?" Vail shakes his head. He is always being accosted by policemen or fringers. Why can't he be accosted by somebody clean and prosperous and well-attired,—somebody with a jewelled ring, say, or a fat black shiny car?

"John, isn't it?" He is thin and shabby and exuberant, the narrow ridge of his nose criss-crossed by broken purple veins. "It is John, isn't it?"

Vail is about to say no,—

"Copy man at Benton & Bowles. I must be right. '78–'79 or thereabouts. Danish Dairy Products. Cushionflor. Callard and Bowser. Or was that Doyle, Dane & Bernbach '77? Might have been. Never can remember. You get them confused, don't you, switching around year after year?" The man shoots his hand out. "Rarity. Pete. You can't have forgotten Pete Rarity. PR. Had my pisser pulled about that more than once. How are you, John, you're looking pretty fucking awful, but who isn't these days, eh?"

7

Vail shakes his head instead of the man's hand and says, "I'm not a copy man." What *is* a copy man?

"Not now you're not," says Pete Rarity. "You're like the rest of us now, eh? In the same boat. Sink or swim. Up the creek paddleless. Always was a dab hand at the sustained metaphor. No, seriously, I get the picture, I know the story. You don't have to lay it on *me*, friend."

Vail says, "I can't somehow help feeling you've made a mistake. I've never worked for any of the companies you mention. Yes, I am out of work, as, judging by appearances, are you. In any case I'm not from around here; never worked in London, in fact."

But of course this doesn't disconcert Pete Rarity one bit. He is the type of person who talks without ever listening to himself. Words are puffs of air, otiose, expendable. In one ear and out the other.

"What are you doing these days?"

"I have several plans. Nothing definite," Vail says cagily. "Nothing decided." (You have to be careful with casual acquaintances; there are *gwiches* everywhere who would sell their grannies for a yellow card or a Resident Alien permit.)

"Fancy a drink?"

"I haven't any money."

Pete Rarity winks a bloodshot eye. "Trust Forte. Got my SS today."

"Not milk."

"I'm flush. Come on."

They walk through the crowded noontime streets, Vail keeping a sharp eye for police, Pete Rarity endlessly talking to fill the vacuum inside his head (Pete Rarity abhors a vacuum). A newspaper placard reads: LEAK SCARE AT DUNGENESS B. The town is crawling with Germans, Swedes, Japanese and Yanks. Men in loosened ties with lightweight jackets draped over their shirtsleeved arms are coming out of pubs. There are the usual number of braless women. The activity is stupefying.

What Vail can't figure out is this: where does the wealth come from? All these people are parasites, non-producers, using up

8

space and resources, and yet by some miracle they continue to exist and thrive and prosper without any visible means of support (braless women!). The manufacturing base is gone, wiped out, he knows that, and with it the underpinning of the economy. Yet money is everywhere on brash vulgar display. It reminds him of a cardboard ocean liner with all lights blazing and a ragged dark brown stain seeping soggily upwards past the lower port-holes whose circles resemble dim green glow-worms shining through the viscous submarine gloom.

A nudge from Pete Rarity,—"Look, Jimmy Tarbuck!"

It is indeed the famous Liverpool comedian riding past in a ghostly silver-grey Rolls-Royce with tinted windows, polished feet propped up on a tasselled cushion, a crystal tumbler of some pale amber liquid in his bejewelled hand, smoking a torpedo-like cigar.

"He told a great joke once," Pete Rarity informs Vail. "Forget what it was now."

[4]

Vail is thirsty and his feet hurt. They pass several establishments where coffee is available but Pete Rarity doesn't suggest stopping at any of them and Vail is too timid and penniless to bring up the subject himself. What is he looking for, the cheapest cup of coffee in London? A topless coffee shop? Health coffee made out of roasted caribou droppings?

On Brewer Street Pete Rarity asks Vail if he'd like to see a live porn show. Vail doesn't express a preference either way. A pair of flabby pockmarked thighs will look the same here as anywhere else, he supposes.

"The coffee is free."

They go down some thinly carpeted stairs and enter a gloomy cavern. They help themselves to a polystyrene cup of machine-dispensed coffee (Vail's black) and sit in the eight-wide cinema-style seating which fills the room wall to wall. The entire row rocks and creaks as the man at the end masturbates under his raincoat. The show hasn't started yet. Half Vail's coffee slops over his hand.

"What made you leave B&B John? Phased rationalisation? Voluntary redundancy? Premature retirement?"

"Not me. I told you that."

"Must have been your bloody twin. Could have sworn . . . same dark eyes. Same black hair,—but not thinning like yours is. A lot of semen shot into the lavatory bowl since then though, eh?" Vail shrugs. "You remind me a bit of Jack Nicholson. You've got Jack Nicholson's hands. Slender, dark-haired, expressive. Though his aren't blue."

Vail looks at his hands, pitted with blister scars. He wonders whether he ought to reply in kind to this flattery and decides not to. Which is just as well, because Pete Rarity does not have a very prepossessing exterior. Far from it. Pinched narrow face with hard spatular chin and sucked-in mouth as if the gums were receding and quick beady bird-like eyes that are never still. This bird-like impression extends to his thin-ridged beaky purple nose.

Pete Rarity drops the crushed polystyrene cup between his bony knees and puts his hand onto Vail's empty groin.

The seats rock and creak.

If it is really true, as Vail reflects, that he is the spitting image of the copy man at B&B, might this not, in one way or another, by some deviously plotted strategem, present itself as an Opportunity?

Not so long ago he had had a past, a green van with a faulty transmission, a wife and child beyond the wire. The memory beckoned to him seductively like lust. Even now inside his own head it was compact and complete, unimpeachable. He could recall many things with absolute sharpness of clarity. The doctor's grey insubstantial presence in the room with the hard chairs and uncurtained window. The limp tartan blanket in his arms, dear to him as breath . . .

Obscurely he felt betrayed, not knowing by what. The scales hadn't completely fallen from his eyes; his thoughts were still confused. The taint of corruption and decay was everywhere,

10

interfering with his senses. He still had, however, his intention, his resolve,—the good deed in the naughty world,—to carry out the supreme act of retribution. That at least, alone, was safe.

Pete Rarity says, "The smell of urine in here makes me sick."

The street is quite as crowded as before: drunks and addicts slump in doorways. The police leave the area unmolested because it is better to contain a cess-pool than have it spilling all over the place and contaminating everything else.

[*With his scant knowledge of London Vail thinks this scene of degradation and despoliation is typical, whereas it isn't, just symptomatic.*]

Men and women of both sexes parade up and down selling orifices. You can buy any shape, size and combination of orifices you fancy here for a few quid. Some of these suck you in while others secrete fluid, depending on whether you want to be swallowed whole or spat upon. In some dank booths you insert a coin and press your face to a cardboard slot and watch a black girl cavort her hips to the disco-throb of a transistor. She pushes sweating flanks close enough to smell and invites you with a moist erect finger to feed in more money if you want to see her have a *really* good time. For paper she will go berserk.

They walk through the sweltering city with no particular destination in mind. It is the height of summer and those with yellow cards are making money hand over fist. The feeling in the air is that the country is booming like never before: video shops going full blast, 5th generation microprocessors selling like there's no tomorrow, Oxford Street thronged, millions of square metres of denim hanging stiffly on plastic rails before being stretched and pummelled to accommodate bulging beef-fattened flesh (a manufacturing base, hoop-la!) while the cars negotiating the choked streets and parked amongst the detritus on buckled pavements are sleek and shiny under their coating of electrostatic dust. The restaurants and pubs are doing a roaring trade, the theatres are packing them (foreigners) in, there is so much frenetic activity and consumption that you wonder how the sewers can cope with it all. Vail has not seen the like in all his thirty-seven years.

11

The intersection of Foley Street and Cleveland Street is sterile, cordoned off because of a bomb blast. This is in the vicinity of a hospital, so the theory goes that somebody of importance receiving treatment there was a marked target. Who can it be? Did the terrorists get the VIP? Imagine killing hundreds of "innocent" people in order to dispose of just the one individual.

Vail would like to poke his nose in to find out how it's done but one glance at the mirrored visors and blunt black stun sticks is enough to warn him off. In any case this method is too crude and indiscriminate; he prefers the intimacy and accuracy of direct confrontation, the inexorability of having the target in his sights and making deadly sure of the outcome.

"Would you like to meet a friend of mine?" Pete Rarity asks him. "He's a producer at Thames. Lives in Notting Hill. Keeps open house. If we're lucky we can get a meal on his expense account. We were at school together and he must be making thirty K a year. He's kept his nose clean, adopted a low profile, and consequently they trust him. Might even get a bed for the night. Better than any old soapbox."

They make their way via Knightsbridge and through the barricades catch a glimpse of workmen swarming over scaffolding in the latest phase of the Harrods' rebuilding programme. Signs curlicued with barbed wire proclaim proudly *We Never Close* and *Business As Usual* in the grand British tradition.

Notting Hill is quiet and riotless these days since the ghettoes were broken up. Families still live in the burnt-out boarded-up shells and fragant cooking smells of braised rat emanate from the gratings.

Everything is peace and harmony.

[5]

The producer who keeps a low profile at Thames for thirty K a year is in his middle thirties, tallish, thinnish, with John Lennon wire-frame spectacles wrapped around large pale ears. Short fine

12

hair brushed forward like a cap over a bony protruding forehead, the veins in his temples resembling blue bulbous worms throbbing beneath a millimetre of pale soil. In speech he is rapid and staccato, in manner brusque and buzzing with nervous energy, as if it is a constant struggle to keep pace with the fleeting moment. He isn't fond of Pete Rarity and, by association, is suspicious of Vail.

For his part, Vail can make out only about one word in ten from the stuttering blizzard of sentences, and no sense at all.

"Fast overrun tight schedule. Damn rewind fucking VTR edit. Silicone pricks. Take studio time and wrap-up ridiculous. Even they couldn't if he tried. But partly Kenny's fault, see to trouble dumb for must, drink or money."

[*An accurate verbatim transcript would have sounded like this to Vail's ears. Yet Pete Rarity appears to have no trouble understanding him: indeed he responds with a toadying question to which Bryce Ransom replies:*]

"Replaced scheduled transmission twats. If network clash Week 14 we didn't sense but hasn't instead? No. They couldn't lick elbow over arse with following wind."

"What's Kenny like to work with?"

"Nothing fired-up didn't have the nous to string it. Could but didn't so bloody sure not. After all, as if he notched 17.9!"

"Didn't he?"

"If seventeen's max then slip in wet uptight cunts. Not in jolly with Vere, though. He's filleted."

Pete Rarity nods sagely in the most servile manner imaginable. Has he understood this gobbledygook? Vail wonders mutely. If not, it is a valiant attempt and successful pretence at same.

Is this how all television producers talk? Or only at Thames? How do people underneath them understand what's to be done, or doesn't it matter? Is it a positive benefit, an essential attribute for the job, to be totally unintelligible to everyone else, particularly those to whom they are supposed to be giving orders?

These questions plague Vail, though never having been near a television studio he can only surmise in ignorance.

Apparently,—missed by Vail in the staccato blizzard,—Bryce Ransom,—Bry to his friends,—has asked them to stay to dinner.

Pete Rarity accepts on Vail's behalf, though it isn't dinner they've been asked to stay for at all, but a party of sorts. Other people appear in the top-floor flat. A supply of tall willowy girls with long straight hair the colour of a SunSilk commercial that cascades over, and is separated by, their pointed shoulders so that golden sheaves fall fore and aft. All these girls are beautiful and refined and speak so slowly and correctly that Vail has time to boil an egg between sentences. They speak to his face as into an empty cardboard box. They have lovely teeth and sweet breaths and tiny pinched nostrils.

Somebody brings news of the hospital carnage involving the INLA (thirty dead, lots more injured) but luckily the Minister for Media and Tabloids was in his missile-proof lead-lined private room on the tenth floor and escaped without a scratch. This, then, clearly isn't the way to set about it (as his instincts had told him). If the Inner London Education Authority can't succeed, what chance has he?

Vail mingles, keeping an ear open for hints and possible openings. There are several men wearing thin gold chains and Adidas training shoes, one or two as slender as the girls. Pete Rarity winks at him from across the room and gives him the thumbs-up. The place reeks of red wine and asparagus quiche. Vail hears an American accent which he is familiar with from TV but has hardly, if ever, heard in the flesh before; it is like being in a B movie.

"Weird Ache," says the American thrusting out a brown fist.

"Pardon?"

"Your name?"

Vail tells him and the American says, "Veal?"

"Vail."

"Vole?"

"*Vail.*"

"Vail. Right. Weird Ache."

"Weird Ache?"

"Wayde. Dake."

"How do you do, Mr Dake."

"Weird."

"Wayde."

"You're into . . . ?"

"Into?"

"What do you do?"

"Me? I'm in video."

"Conception, production or packaging?"

"Integrate following let who fucks who tight, wouldn't they," says Vail, taking a leaf out of Bry's book. It seems to work; the American nods vigorously. "Too damn right. Somebody has to."

"What are you in?"

"Excuse me?"

"What do you do?"

"CP/M security and surveillance." He proffers a card. "Need an ALU, BCD, LSI or LCD and I'm your man. We can interface any number of peripherals and give you a menu, modem, matrix, or mouse. Pick a random number and we can scroll it, synthesise it, simulate it, spreadsheet it, sprite it and stack it."

"All at once?"

"Yep or sequentially. Don't forget, the world is running to a dead end. We have to speed up the process."

"I thought we had to slow it down?"

"*No*. You've got to stay one kilobyte ahead. Tomorrow's advance is yesterday's stale fish. *Be* there."

"I'm not up with all this, I'm afraid."

"We can help. Outfit you with PEEK, PROM and POKE and you'll fly like a turtle. You'll never look back," the American avers.

Now. This looks promising. This could be a way in. If he can get hold of a security and surveillance system there's no telling where it might lead,—not to mention the PEEKs, PROMs and POKEs and other things. He could gain access to all sorts of places:

15

Buckingham Palace, Downing Street, the Houses of Parliament, Harrods. Say he bought a pair of headphones with dangly wires and wore a white coat and wandered in with the rest of the technical crew? Would they spot him? He could mumble CP/M scroll POKE Kbyte and look preoccupied. Nobody ever stopped a man in a white coat who mumbled and looked preoccupied; you could operate on the Queen Mother if you did that, and most of them had.

So Vail sets about to pick the American's brains, who, it transpires, comes from Austin, Texas. He is a massively broad fellow, creased and hard and gnarled as an olive tree, with craggy slits for eyes. His teeth are square white slabs in a mouth as wide as his head. He has a solid moustache burnt yellow by the Texas sun. It seems he will accede to Vail's request for CP/M security and surveillance information if he (Vail) will arrange to have one of the tall willowy correctly-spoken girls spend the night with him (Dake).

He must think I'm an old friend of Bry's, thinks Vail, *with some kind of influence over the people here. What should I do? And if I agree, how do I arrange for one of the girls to spend the night with him? They won't look at me anyway, for myself, much less as a go-between or sexual intermediary. Wouldn't you think too that a broad tanned rich American (all Americans are rich) would have a far greater chance of pulling a bird than a specimen like me? Unless the American supposes there is some significant difference between American girls and English girls, that a different approach is required, and he (Wayde Dake) feels insecure in dealing with females of an alien culture,—for all his wealth and aplomb and slick expertise in security and surveillance systems unsure which social and emotional triggers to press to activate the desired response.*

"I know all about that," says Wayde Dake, having read Vail's mind, "and much of it is true, partly anyway. Will you give it your best shot? I'd be appreciative."

"I'll do the best I can," Vail promises, his mind agog with openings and opportunities.

The party has speeded up considerably as more people arrive in droves. Outside the streets lurk with unmitigated violence and squalor; here in the top-floor flat it is hot, oppressive, fume-laden, noisy with conversation and shrieks and thumping disco-throb. Drugs are taken, weed smoked, smack inhaled.

Bryce Ransom pauses to have a brief chat with Vail but the result is as incomprehensible and inconclusive as before. His verbal bullets spatter Vail's face, eyes crinkling astutely behind his twisted wire-frame specs, exposed bony temples writhing with wormy blue veins.

It crosses Vail's mind to wonder whether this isn't a deliberate ploy. The motive? To see how many people pretend to understand because they don't wish to offend a television producer, thereby affording much secret amusement to Bryce Ransom as well as being an instant litmus test of the cretinous, the gullible, the sycophantic: in other words those prepared to debase themselves to the *nth* degree in order to win the favour and approbation of an important personage. What a clever wheeze! Laughing up his sleeve at the world while passing off a spate of gibberish as incisive intellectual pyrotechnics. You have to admire the fellow, though Vail doesn't, finding him tiresome.

But,—this Vail's banal perplexity,—how does the producer from Thames go about buying groceries or ordering a meal in a restaurant? Is it all done by gesture and dumb show? ESP? Semaphore?

It seems sound policy to concentrate on one girl in particular. Besides, he can't talk to them all at once, it would be too confusing.

For a tall willowy blonde English girl Angela is extraordinarily short, dumpy, dark-haired and Australian. She works as an editor for BBC Publications, speaks with an Aussie accent and prefers to be called Angie. Vail enters into conversation with Angie by the simple expedient of overhearing a reference to an author called

John Folwes and expressing his liking of and admiration for said author's works, even though he has never read a single word John Folwes has written, much less heard of him.

There follows an animated dialogue concerning Folwes which Vail, for his part, makes up as he goes along. Angie doesn't appear to notice any glaring omission or discrepancy: apparently Folwes is an author you can discuss in considerable depth without ever having read a line.

But Angie has read all his works, some of them several times over in the continuing search for a meaning to life, and in Vail believes she has found a like mind, a soul-mate, of course exemplified by their shared literary taste. Expressing an admiration for Folwes, Vail discovers, is like belonging to an exclusive club or society whose members wear revolving beacons on top of their heads. You can easily spot them fifty metres across a crowded room and, should you be so minded, home in like a motorway sparrow hawk pouncing on a small furry rodent.

Thus it is that in a cramped corner next to a rubber plant and a Munch woodcut reproduction in a stainless steel frame on an off-white rough-cast wall, pushed chest to chest by the crush and holding their glasses of wine underneath their chins, they explore the labyrinthine symbolism and essential message of Folwes while their eyes delve into the murky hidden recesses of the other, noting in passing his unshaven paleness, lined mouth and blank grey eyes and her brown freckled skin and small breasts with dark prominent nipples.

The din and clatter all around shrinks to a blur of sound; the music heard as a reverberation through the soles of their feet; the wine and heat and sensual attraction swimming in their heads like lazy goldfish.

"Have you noticed that people at parties seem to have no past?"

Vail nods, then shakes his head. No, he never has.

"Well," Angie says, licking wine from her upper lip. "They

18

arrive out of nowhere,—literally. Materialise from the abyss. Know what I mean? As though they've been instantly created for the occasion. Normally they're kept stacked flat in airless storerooms and only brought out and assembled and arranged about the place as required,—like those kids' pop-up books which as you turn a page erect themselves into a scene complete with people and furniture.

"I mean, think about it:

"All these people turn up here tonight, who you've never seen before, and it takes a supreme effort of imagination to convince yourself that their lives were going on before you laid eyes on them. Well, doesn't it? They were created the instant they walked in. Never existed before,—stacked flat in airless storerooms.

"Take the extremely tall guy over there with the spotted bald head, pink glasses and velvet bow tie. He's just this minute been invented! He doesn't exist at any other time! Impossible to believe he got out of bed this morning, had a wash, ate his breakfast of muesli and toast, ran for the train at Sutton, arrived at the office, had a stand-up lunch in the pub (cheese and pickle sandwich, half a lager), went back to work, so on and so forth.

"Even you,—or me," Angie goes on and on, gazing up fiercely into his eyes. "We're like characters in a novel who only come into being the moment the author sets pen to paper. They have no past, and neither, for one another, do we. We could be stricken out by a swipe of the pen. I don't believe you have a past and you don't believe I have one either. Why, until just a few minutes ago you didn't even know I existed,—and I didn't!"

Vail wafts himself, saying, "It's very hot in here," not knowing what else to say. (He was doing great with Folwes, holding his own, but events seem to have taken a turn for the worse. Is he meant to respond to this, and, if so, with what?)

"For all you know I could be one of the ready-made people stacked flat in an airless storeroom just waiting to be assembled!" —triumphant!

"Well, yes," Vail is prepared to concede, not entirely sure where this gets them. "You could be." Angie might be fictitious (even

19

though she works for the BBC) but his own past is inviolate. He knows full well where he came from and precisely where,—sidetracks, dead ends, wrong turnings notwithstanding,—he's going.

Somewhere the Opportunity lies in wait for him. It might come from any direction, from any slight quirk of events or random juxtaposition of circumstances. He is prepared to explore all possibilities.

Already, in the space of a few hours, a number of interesting avenues have been revealed, come to light, as it were:

1. He has been mistaken for a copy man.

2. He has become acquainted with an incomprehensible television producer.

3. An American has asked a favour of him in exchange for certain information.

4. An Australian girl with small breasts and dark prominent nipples has come into his life.

For a fictitious character Vail reckons he is doing all right.

[6]

In the normal course of events there ought to be a sex scene here between Vail and a tall blonde willowy English girl who happens to be small, dark-haired, Australian and works for the BBC.

We can all imagine such a scene for ourselves. It will no doubt feature certain named portions of male and female anatomy, quiescent and in motion; it will be either soft and rapturous or hard and brutal, or possibly a combination of both. He (Vail) will perform certain acts upon her (Angie) and she will reciprocate in kind, insofar as their physical dissimilarities allow. There might even be net curtains billowing gently in the humid breeze (it is a hot night, remember) and soft-focus prose about heaving mounds and entwining limbs and sheens of reflected light on damp skin. It might also include, God forbid, elements of erect allegory and limp symbolism.

Instead of this titillating sideshow let us press on.

Some women like to know everything there is to know about a man, and the more he goes against the grain, the more he fails to fit or resists the accepted patterns of behaviour, the more insatiably voracious they become in pursuit of knowledge, to possess him, control him. Perhaps Angie is attracted to strays and fringers, who knows? At any rate she finds him "interesting", a man with a mysterious and alluring past, and this because of rather than despite his long and matted hair, crumpled evil-smelling clothes, the hollow defeated look about him, especially noticable in the sag of his cheeks and the puffy dark bags under his eyes.

Even the difference in ages,—Angie is twenty-three,—could be said to be another factor in his favour: a further disparity, departure from the norm, which excites her worst dark thrilling suspicions.

They leave the party and go back to her room, which isn't very far away (Sheffield Terrace), walking through the prowling streets after midnight, a risky thing to do in this day and age. She makes coffee (no milk for Vail) and they listen to a black singer called Joan Armourtrading while Angie sits cross-legged in the classic pose at Vail's disreputable feet, her small round face upturned attentively, dark eyes watching his mouth, comfortable in the knowledge that he is to stay the night and therefore happy that the sexual potency quivering in the air between them will be discharged in good time, leaving only an interim period to be filled with pleasant non-combative conversation.

"I get so *depressed*," Angie tells him, "looking for a deeper meaning to life. There must be one and yet I can't find it."

"Where have you looked?"

"Everywhere."

"At the BBC?"

"In Australia, at the BBC, sitting on the lavatory, *everywhere*."

To Vail she sounds desperate and at the same time complacent, as if looking and not finding a deeper meaning to life is an enviable state to be in; smug confirmation of one's proper intellectual status.

"There must be more to it than *this*," Angie goes on with some vehemence. "I mean, look at it. Orthodox religion up shit creek, we're poisoning ourselves with toxic waste, Dallas has more murders per year than England and Wales combined, the universe is expanding out of control, you can't get fresh milk delivered to your doorstep any more, we're slaughtering baby seals to make eyeshadow, leaded petrol is making children into morons, we've stockpiled enough nukes to kill every man, woman and child on the planet fifty times over, billions of people are starving in the Third World, you can't walk down the street without being grabbed and raped, in Russia they put dissidents into psychiatric wards and pump them full of Majetpil, we force-feed animals to get a juicy steak, there's too much violence and pornography on television, entropy is increasing exponentially, you can't get a decent meal in a restaurant under £20, they're chopping down all the trees in the Amazonian Basin, everybody's in it for what they can get, the trains are filthy and don't run on time, you can't go outside the wire without getting shot, old people die of hypothermia, people spend more on gambling than they do on health care, wives are being battered, there's less than ten per cent real meat in sausages, shoals of haddock have been wiped out by nuclear runoff,—"

Vail ventures a timely interruption.

"I think it is true that one gains a certain hold on sausages and haddock by writing them down."

"You do?"

"Yes."

"I wouldn't know about that,—all I know is that I'm sick to death. Everyone thinks it's wonderful working at the BBC but it isn't. For from it. The canteen meals are disgusting. I gave better slop to my dingo back in Perth."

22

Vail says, "You've got your yellow card and you're not plagued by *gwiches*."

Angie's interest perks up at once. "Did a *gwich* ever shop you?"

"Not yet. But I have to be careful."

Her eyes gleam. "Because you haven't got a yellow card?"

"That could be one reason," Vail says carefully.

"The others?"

Vail examines his dirty nails.

"I won't mind if you don't tell me but I'd love to know,—have you killed somebody?" Parted wet lips breathless.

"No of course not," Vail says immediately.

"Swindled the SS?"

"Not yet."

"This is like a guessing game. Er, let me see,—you handle drugs and hard-core porn."

Vail holds up both arms and looks from one threadbare sleeve to the other.

"No, I guess you don't. I give up. What do they want you for? What have you done?" Her hand creeps underneath her dress and along her inner thigh. "Something bad? Is it bad? Very bad?"

"What would you like it to be?"

Angie inserts the tips of two fingers into her vagina and slides them up and down. "I bet it's something really nasty, isn't it? A horrible sex crime." She rocks slowly back and forth, a flush entering her cheeks. "What I think you did was to get a young innocent schoolgirl and force her to undergo certain perverse practises. Made her hold it, I bet, and masturbate you, sticking up in front of her face, veined and swollen, didn't you?" She holds her breath for a moment and lets go a whimper. "And when it started to pulsate you aimed it right into her face, I bet, didn't you, and made her keep wanking you harder and harder till you shot it all over her perfect rosebud mouth." She moans softly, breathing fast and shuddery, and expels all her breath at once and falls back onto the rug, eyes shut, legs splayed.

"If you like," Vail says, unmoved. "In fact it's nothing like that."

There is a law operating somewhere in the universe to the effect that unconnected events and random happenings conglomerate arbitrarily around a common centre.

[*Vail doesn't know why this is, simply feels it to be true.*]

Having rid herself of the ache in her loins (seeking a meaning to life in masturbatory fantasies concerning older disreputable men with mysterious, alluring pasts) Angie is prepared to listen to him in a calmer frame of mind. She still finds him intriguing even though the pulse of bloodheat has ceased to beat; if anything the fact that he could sit so dispassionately has sharpened her curiosity about this shagged-out empty-groined masturbation-watcher. She had come so quickly that it even took her sliding fingers by surprise.

She makes fresh coffee and resettles herself on the rug at his feet. "Do you know where to begin?" Angie asks him.

"I think so," Vail replies. "Do you want to hear it all?"

"Every last word."

"Parts of it are fixed in my brain while others are patchy and hazy. But I'll do my best."

24

2ND SECTION   MOTORWAY (I)

There were three of us in the Bedford 22cwt van,—Mira, Bev and me,—and we'd already broken down twice between Zuttor Estate and junction 19 of the M62: the tremendous distance of six miles. The second breakdown happened on the gently declining slip road leading onto the motorway itself. I was underneath the van with an adjustable spanner trying to loosen something that had seized up when the black boots and leggings of a motorcycle policeman came into view and plonked themselves about eighteen inches from my oil-smeared nose. A bass rumble of a voice, and I heard Mira reply, "I don't know. Overheated I think. We'll get it going, we have before." Not very smart. The policeman would get the idea it was a regular occurrence (which it was) and have us towed away to the scrapyard. Lying on my back I prayed that he wouldn't ask to see the MOT test certificate, which I didn't possess, having bought the van from a Pakistani who wanted £250 but settled for £200 because the van didn't have its MOT. Wisely, I stayed where I was and let Mira work her feminine charm on the policeman. She was good at this, being an attractive woman with a warm smile and sympathetic manner, both of which were natural and unforced. She was also well blessed in the bust department.

I tinkered and banged ineffectually while the conversation went on above me. I could see the receding curvature of the green van and Mira's pinpoint head poking out of the driver's window as reflected in the polished toe-cap of the policeman's left boot. Around it little dancing waves of air shimmered off the hot tarmac. In the toe-cap I saw the white blob of his helmet swell alarmingly as he bent on one knee and his brown moustached face appeared sideways underneath the rusting exhaust pipe, tinted goggles clinging to his helmet like limpets to a rock.

25

"Where are you optimistically hoping to get in this?"

"Lancaster."

"You're pointing the wrong way."

"We want to get on the M6."

"And then go north?" I nodded. "Think you'll make it?"

"It's nothing serious. It seizes up with the heat."

"Have you got an MOT for this heap?"

I nodded again.

He gazed straight at me.

I started to edge towards his polished boot, making as if to get out, grunting and grimacing to suggest it was ten times harder than it was.

"Okay, all right, forget it, but don't take all day. I don't want you here when I come back in an hour. One hour."

"No danger of that, officer."

"There'd better bloody not be, chum."

I had paid the homage of obeisance and he went away satisfied, virility unbesmirched.

It would be about forty minutes later that we were on the M6 heading south. The engine gave out a pounding oily roar beneath me, shaking the steering wheel and making my fingers numb. Mira was in the back with Bev, who was lying down covered with a blanket. We didn't know what was wrong with her. She had been sickening for something for months now and the doctor had put her on the waiting-list for a specialist to examine her, though he couldn't promise anything or say when it was likely to be. He could get her into Fairfield Clinic right away, that same day, but there wasn't much chance of that; we were six weeks behind on the rent for our two-bedroom broom closet on Zuttor Estate as it was, and threatened with eviction, which was why we were hightailing it down the M6 in a clapped-out Bedford van with a faulty transmission.

Fortunately the policeman hadn't seen any of our papers (including the non-existent MOT certificate), and so wouldn't be able to recall our name when it came up on the list of corporation absconders.

26

That little piece of luck seemed a good omen. Almost but not quite made me forget how much I wanted a drink. I had a bottle stashed away somewhere but to have gone for it would have caused such a blazing row followed by a sulky black silence that I preferred to suffer stoically in the cause of peace. Another bonus was that the vibrating wheel successfully camouflaged the tremor in my hands.

Mira, feet straddled apart to steady herself, leaned over my shoulder to offer a thermos of coffee. I almost spilt it and still managed to dribble some of the coffee down my chin, caused by the thread inside the cup which interfered with the smooth purchase of my lips to the plastic rim.

"What about petrol?"

"What about it?" I said, handing the cup back.

"Don't be like that."

"I'm not being like anything."

"Then just answer me in a civil manner."

"What do you want to know?"

"What are we going to do about petrol? Have you any money? I haven't any money. I've got a couple of pounds to last us; get Bev something at a service station. I've no money for petrol."

"What do you have to get her? We've got food."

"Cheese and corned beef sandwiches and crisps aren't going to last forever. This is the only liquid we've got. We'll need drinks."

"For two pounds you'll be lucky to get two coffees and a glass of weak lemonade."

"Don't start, Jack. I'm not going through it all again, I warn you! You can piss off!"

"We're all pissing off," I said. "To the affluent slumbering south."

"That's if we make it."

"We'll make it." My right foot was numb from the pressure of keeping the accelerator flat to the floor; even so we were hardly touching forty, and our speed was gradually falling mile by mile.

27

"On fresh air?" Mira said sardonically.

When she was in this mood I could have belted her. "Don't worry about it. Leave it to me."

"Leave it to you," Mira said. "Recipe for disaster. If I left it to you, Jack, Bev and me would be in the poorhouse and you'd be in prison."

She snorted her famous laugh: harsh, derisory, acrimonious.

The heat and fumes from the engine were making me dizzy. My hands were slippery on the wheel. A sign said: Holmes Chapel Services 3 miles. If Mira took Bev to the lavatory I could sneak a crafty swig and think up a way to get some petrol. Mira was right, we were nearly empty. She was humming a childhood song to comfort Bev. I vaguely recalled the words: "Thank you for the food we eat, thank you for the world so sweet . . ."

I parked some distance away from the main building to give them a longer walk and me more time. There were more wrecks and write-offs than I expected. The grass verges were strewn with old ripped tyres and bits of engines, the odd buckled door panel, smashed wing mirrors, and everywhere broken glass.

On the other side of the perimeter road there was an encampment of families living in junked vehicles and boarded-up caravans, kids running around with sooty faces from the oily fires which had black-bottomed pans and cooking pots slung over them from wires and metal brackets. Whatever they were cooking it smelled good.

I took a couple of hefty slugs and stowed the bottle away. I was past caring whether or not Mira caught a whiff of it on my breath. I stood in the sunshine feeling the tremor pass away from my hands and the backs of my knees, looking over the hot wavering roofs of cars to the Rolls and Mercs and BMWs behind electrified fencing in the VIP compound. Some of them came with motorcycle outriders dressed all in black, bulbous visored helmets reflecting the sun like the hard carapaces of shiny black beetles. George Lucas might have dreamed them up for *Star Wars VII*.

I tried to guess who the people travelling in the armoured limousines might be. TV personalities? Pop stars? Company

28

directors? Politicians? Deejays? Stockbrokers? Fashion designers? Advertising executives? Record company producers? Film people? Industrialists? Official receivers? Chat show hosts? Washing powder tycoons? Video pirates? Slum landlords? Oil magnates? Trade union leaders? Prostitutes? BBC chiefs? Jingle writers? International financiers? Swindlers? Merchant bankers? Best-selling novelists? Sports stars? Arms salesmen?

A tanned voluptuous blonde girl came out of the VIP building flanked by two swarthy men wearing dark glasses and tailored suits. She had on a low-cut dress with a silver fox fur draped across her shoulders and snaking through the scented crooks of her elbows.

I thought I recognised her as Selina Southorn, a video porn starlet who reputedly (I'd never seen any of her movies) could wink at the camera while at the same time extinguishing a candle from across the room. She was currently featured in a TV commercial, blowing kisses to promote the properties of patented self-sealing red rubber seals for kilner jars.

From the back of the van I took out an empty oil can and a length of rubber hose. Another advantage of being parked away from the main building was that there were fewer people about. Most cars had locks on their petrol caps, but I only needed to find one that hadn't, and after a bit of stealthy loping found a Lancia with corroded bodywork conveniently parked with its rear end next to a low wall which enabled me to siphon off a couple of gallons unobserved. I did two more trips and emptied the tank completely.

This stealing of non-renewable fossil fuel resources was a risky business. Nearly every day you read in the paper about somebody caught in illegal possession of oil, coal or gas; in fact the black economy thrived on these commodities. The usual sentence was a minimum of ten years hard, though some were summarily executed on the spot. Only a month or two ago a friend of mine on Zuttor had been lucky enough to escape a mob lynching for lifting a bottle of Calor.

"It's like a refugee camp," Mira said when she returned with

29

Bev. "People sprawled out in the corridors and all over the stairs. They ought to do something."

"What?" I said. "Gas them or put them in prison you mean?"

"Don't ask me. The place reeks."

I asked Bev how she was feeling. In fact she looked terrible. She had scratched the sores on her face and neck raw. The doctor had given Mira some yellow ointment to dab on which didn't do anything, not even stop the sores itching and weeping. Generally she looked pale and thin and washed out.

Mira noticed but offered no comment on the fuel gauge miraculously registering half-full and I didn't bother to explain. Near Crewe we passed a YOP (Young Offenders Party) in grey overalls digging up the hard shoulder in the hot sunshine. You could see the purple numbers tattooed on the backs of their shaved heads. Some of them, I suppose, were no more than twelve or thirteen, probably inside for chasing the dragon.

Mira said, "I'm sorry if I was a bit snappish earlier on," placing her hand on my shoulder. She leaned her head closer and I was conscious of the fumes on my breath. "We should stick together, not fall out."

I nodded without speaking, staring straight ahead through the windscreen spattered with the blood and guts of insects.

"I'm worried about Bev."

"Me too."

Mira was usually a sensible level-headed person, which made this a startling, even shocking, admission on her part. I laughed.

"It's a kids' complaint, not the bubonic plague," I said. "A good doctor will sort her out in no time once we get to London. A dose of antibiotics and some proper nursing care." I believed this at the time; the thought that Bev might die had never entered my head.

Mira's arm stiffened and withdrew. "I can smell whisky. Where did you get the money for booze?"

"I borrowed it."

"Liar. Who'd lend you money?"

"I sold my binoculars."

"How much for?"

"Nine pounds."

"Nine? *Nine?* They cost you forty-five!" She snorted. "To one of your drinking pals, I suppose."

I kept tight hold of the wheel, my foot aching from the constant pressure of keeping the pedal flat down to the floor; even so our speed was edging lower by imperceptible degrees as the engine overheated. How far to the next service station?

"Was it?"

"Was it what?"

"To one of your boozing cronies?"

"Does it matter? I got nine pounds for them."

"And spent it all on whisky. You knew we needed that money. You bloody lousy stinking sod. You selfish unfeeling bastard,—"

"I thought we were going to stick together and not fall out."

"Your own daughter is seriously ill and you go and spend money on drink,—you weak thoughtless pig. No thought for Bev!"

"Nine pounds wouldn't have paid for a bedpan in Fairfield Clinic."

"It would have bought food and petrol!"

"We're on the road, aren't we? The van is moving, isn't it?"

Her voice went flat and hard. "I'm finished with you, Jack. That is it. Finished."

"Shall I drop you here or at the next service stat?"

"You're so bloody clever, aren't you? Jack bloody know-it-all Vail."

The conversation went on, desultorily, in this vein for a few more miles while our speed died away until we were nudging no more than 20 mph. A convoy of army lorries and armoured half-tracks, lights blazing, overtook us, sturdy bronzed young men in voluminous camouflage drill noting our snail's progress with patronising indifference on their torpid moon-round beef-fed faces. A machine-gun was set up in the back of one of the lorries, manned by a red-headed soldier with a fledgling moustache making practice sweeps across the three lanes of the motorway.

There was no alternative: we would have to stop to allow the belching green bastard time to cool down. The inside of the cab was like an oven; stripped down as I was to my T-shirt, sweat bathed my chest and ran down from my arm-pits.

I climbed out of my seat and went to have a look at Bev. She was sleeping soundly, her livid suppurating face in repose. Her eyelids were like two raw peeled slugs. At least we couldn't argue, Mira and me, without disturbing her.

"Are you coming outside?"

"No," Mira said. "I'll stay here and watch her." Her eyes were like slits under her streaky gold dark-brown hair which was parted and swept back as if formed into a bow-wave by her wide forehead. "Try not to finish the bottle. I don't think I could drive this thing," she said as I opened the side door and stepped outside.

I walked along the hard shoulder to a concrete culvert built into the embankment. It was cooler here, shielded from the sun, and I was hidden from the motorway. The bottom of the culvert was dry, brittle sticks and bleached stones and gravel piled up into little hillocks by the passage of water. Lower down these dry runnels disappeared into an iron grille which led to a drainage conduit under the motorway itself.

After the third swallow I began to feel blearily benign and lulled by the smear of traffic sliding past. I didn't give a shit what Mira thought and loved her with all my heart. She blamed me for our predicament, which hurt me deeply, because she was right. I felt stricken and ashamed by the knowledge and bitterly defiant,—more, angry, incensed, choked up to boiling point. Worst of all I had lost her respect. I saw myself through her eyes and could hardly bear the agony. Why were women so strong? Their abiding strength was an affront, a perpetual sneer. What had they to be so damned complacent about? True enough, they shouldered all the burdens, took all the crass crap of men with a gently patient smile, were battered and bruised into submission, *and yet were not defeated!* Not only not defeated, but triumphant, victorious. Could you beat that? Could you credit it? What hope was there for the male gender when faced with an indefatigable, accusing, reproachful, infinitely pliant and forbearing enemy such as that? How could you possibly win? Where was the justice in that? Justice? Don't make me laugh.

I took another drink to dilute the tears and a hollow voice said, "I need help and you need help. If you help me I'll help you. Is it a deal?"

The man in the culvert was Urban Brown (his real name I swear, not a made-up one) and he was on the run, you could tell that at once by his face and his shoes. He was wearing a grimy corduroy shirt and filthy jeans with holes in the knees and arse, and carrying a heavy thick black overcoat wrapped into a bundle and tied up with string. He had a triangular sallow face and prominent bones, deep vertical creases in his cheeks, and a dark-blue jawline that could never look clean-shaven even five minutes after the expert attentions of a barber with a cut-throat razor. To categorise him: a starved crafty working-class face: insolent too; harbouring grudges and zealously storing up slights, real and imagined. Like many left-wing activists he was more interested in revenge than equality.

I said, "You must be in a poor way if you need my help."

He almost snarled, "Not for long, friend," and came nearer, crabwise, eyeing the bottle. I gave it to him. He gripped it by the neck as if throttling a chicken and took a powerful gulp, throat muscles working, holding his bundle close under his arm as if it contained either the crown jewels or a spare set of dentures.

"Is that your van?" he asked, handing the bottle back.

I nodded warily. There wasn't a single thing I liked the look of about this character. I'd met his type in bars and always steered well clear of them. They were forever keen to do you favours to their advantage.

"Who's with you?"

"My wife and daughter."

"Just the three of you?"

"Yes, why, are you going to hijack us?"

He didn't bother or even pretend to grin. He said:

"I need transport. I have to get to London. I won't give you any bullshit about my car breaking down, you're an intelligent bloke, you can see that isn't true. The police are after me, that is the

33

truth. I haven't any money either. I'm asking you straight out to help me. Throwing myself on your mercy."

Nobody had ever thrown themselves on my mercy before; it had an antique ring to it that pleased me.

"If I refused you could always use force. Isn't that what desperate men resort to?"

"Not desperate men who haven't eaten for three days."

"Would you consider it otherwise?"

"Yes."

"You are pretty desperate then?"

"To get to London quickly,—yes."

"That's my side of the deal, what's yours?"

He frowned,—almost glowered,—at me suspiciously, his eyes hooded and watchful.

"You said, 'If you help me I'll help you'."

"Oh that. I could tell you things. I know what's going on. Only a few of us know. You won't read it in the papers or see it on TV. There are closely-guarded secrets that the man-in-the-street knows nothing about, would never imagine in his wildest dreams. But I'd tell you."

"Not the ultimate mystery of the pyramids," I said, "or that we're all descended from aliens. I know that already."

Still no grin.

"Secrets like these you could be killed for knowing."

"How come that's a help?"

"Knowledge is power."

"Not if you're dead."

"Forget that. This is the real stuff. I'm not kidding. You'll shit your clogs when you know what it is. You'll be one of the few people who really knows what's going on. That's worth more than a measly trip to London, isn't it?"

I'd met loonies but never a real madman before. Was he mad? He sounded like a freemason. "What have you done?" I asked him. "Robbed a bank or murdered someone?"

He gave me a scathing, sneering grin (at last). "Petty stuff. I plant bombs. I kill people *en masse*. I'm a terrorist."

This was a conversation stopper, particularly in my befuddled state of tertiary intoxication. I suppose I gaped at him.

"I'm Number One on their hit list. They'd love to get their hands on me and stage a show trial. The *Sun* would have a field day."

"By 'they' you mean the police?"

"The authorities. The panoply of the state with its judiciary and law-enforcement tentacles."

(What kind of jargon was this? Panoply and tentacles in the same sentence!)

"Dangerous to boast about it," I suggested.

"I'm not boasting, just stating facts. You want proof?" He tapped the black bundle significantly with long dirt-rimmed nails. "Here."

"Not a bomb?" I said nervously.

"You think I'm stupid?" He shook his head and his eyes narrowed and he leaned forward slightly and mouthed, "Communication."

"Communication," I repeated imbecilically.

"Want to see?"

"No, I'll take your word for it." The less I knew about this, the better. Still, it wasn't every day that one met a terrorist.

Also I was intrigued to learn what these "closely-guarded secrets" were that "the man-in-the-street" knew nothing about. Myself I had often suspected that certain facts were being withheld from the population at large: we were continually being reminded by TV, radio and newspapers that we had a free press, one of the cornerstones of democracy, and yet when you read the "free" press you found that it contained nothing more revelatory than women with their legs spread wide and endless columns of bingo numbers.—Suppose lots of things went on that were either completely suppressed or distorted to give the exact reverse of the truth? If all the media were in collusion (it was possible), there would be no means of ascertaining the real truth except by rumour, hearsay, word-of-mouth, etc.

I stoppered the bottle and took him back to the van. On the way he told me his name, but I decided to introduce him to Mira simply as "Brown" and omit the "Urban", reasoning that it might be safer in the long run. Perfect name for a terrorist, I remember thinking,—Urban Brown,—ordinary, commonplace, yet at the same time unsettling, disquieting, allusive.

Mira was none too pleased. She became monosyllabic and kept catching my eye furiously. I didn't care. I was in her bad books to begin with, so had nothing to lose. If I hadn't been drunk I don't think I would have taken the risk of transporting a known terrorist under the noses of the police, but disposition, curiosity and intoxication had conspired that July day in a sort of giddy recklessness, and here we were, the four of us, heading south down the hot black snake of the M6 in sweltering sunshine. Yipee!!

The Knutsford (Rank) service station I decided to give a miss because we still had a quarter tank of petrol and the next service stat, Sandbach (Road Chef), wasn't all that far and I judged we'd make it before running out of fuel.

It was round about four o'clock now, still hot, which wasn't good for the engine. Constantly pressing the accelerator to the floor had left me with a numb right leg up to the thigh.

Another fear, or worry, made me sweat as much as the heat. Was there a curfew on this section of motorway, and, if so, what was the deadline? To be caught breaking curfew was bad enough, but to be stopped and searched whilst harbouring a fugitive . . . !

Not clever; definitely dumb.

There was a conversation going on in the back that I couldn't hear. Brown was asking questions and Mira was answering him quite animatedly. He said something and I heard her snort with laughter. In the mirror I could see his narrow dark face with its prominent bones and starved eyes brightly illuminated by the golden light slanting through the side windows. He said he had killed people *en masse* and I could believe it. No, not an evil face, I would have said, but fixed, purposive, callous; in a word, ruthless.

I wouldn't like to run into him on a dark night, I remember thinking.

I moved my head to look at Mira in the mirror but the angle was wrong and all I could see was a shoulder and broken white lines converging sharply to a focal point in the distance behind us. Mira snorted again. What the hell was he saying to make her laugh?

I knew I would have to pull the same stunt for petrol at Sandbach that I had employed at Holmes Chapel. Brown would have to stay out of sight. I couldn't risk anyone spotting him. Service stats were crawling with strays and fringers, so his unkempt appearance wouldn't excite comment, but there would be police and possibly the odd *gwich* floating around. It suddenly occurred to me that there might be a reward out for Brown. We could use the money. I hadn't seen any posters with his mug shot and description, though I made a mental note to keep my eyes skinned. Everyone *glaswellted* on everyone else these days and thought nothing of it; it was the prevailing ethic of the times in which we lived.

By tomorrow, I thought, somebody in a nearby flat on Zuttor would have informed the council of our midnight flit. First they would break in and ransack the place, taking everything they could carry, smash it up for good measure, and then collar the rent collector on his rounds and slip him the word in the hope that he wouldn't use the heavy hand on their next default of payment and might even give them a free week. Some people practically existed by informing.

Another snort of laughter, which I ignored. (I hated it when other people,—men I mean,—made Mira snort. The sound came up her windpipe and got stuck behind her epiglottis, where it imploded. It wasn't the sound itself I hated, but the fact that someone else's humour appealed to her whereas mine had long since palled.) What was he *saying*?

I glanced irritably into the mirror, which was filled with a flashing red sign reading POLICE STOP. I took my aching foot off the accelerator and gently pressed the brake pedal, guiding the van onto the hard shoulder.

There were two identikit policemen with thick moustaches and clean shaven lantern jaws and mirror sunglasses. They wore shiny black zippered nylon blousons and peaked caps raised up parabolically at the front and pulled flat across the crown of their heads with thin leather straps, like the Schutzstaffel used to wear. They had gunbelts and bulky black leather holsters bulging with firepower. One came to the driver's window, the other stationed himself by the nearside door towards the rear of the van and peered in inquisitively.

"Where's the funeral?" asked the first policeman sarcastically.

"Fuel pump on the blink, officer. Sorry. I'll get it fixed at Sandbach."

"Licence." He proffered a skin-tight black leather glove which showed the shapes of his knuckles and square-cut fingernails, and I handed him the licence enclosed in its plastic sheath. "Where are you going and why?"

"Birmingham to see relatives. My wife's sister."

"Where are you exiting?"

"Nine."

"Is that your wife in back?"

"Yes."

"Name?"

"Jack."

"Wife's name, dumbo."

"Mira. Sorry."

"Who's that with her?"

"My daughter. Bev."

"We'll look inside."

The first policeman, who had the name HUCK stencilled above his right breast pocket, went round to join the other policeman, who had MUTCH stencilled above his, and they squeezed one after the other through the narrow side door and stood filling the interior of the van with abundant healthy flesh, bowed at the shoulders because their peaked caps grazed the pale green underside of the metal roof.

Their blank mirrored gaze swept everywhere.

"Cosy in here, Tim," said HUCK to MUTCH.

"We'll look through your stuff," MUTCH said to me. "If you've no objection."

"No. None. Please. Look." I had climbed out of my seat and the three of us were stooping together in the hot claustrophobic space. The smell of Brut aftershave was overwhelming.

MUTCH opened a drawer in the sink unit and rattled knives and forks about while HUCK knelt down to pull open the long drawer underneath the bunk on which Bev was lying, hair stuck to her forehead above her red bloated eyelids. HUCK paused with his gloved hands on the recessed handles and shied back from the waist. "She looks sick."

"She does, doesn't she?"

"What's wrong with her?"

I shrugged from my crouch. "No idea. The doctors are baffled. She has a temperature and can't keep anything down. Your guess is as good as mine."

"What's the problem, Fred?" MUTCH asked, his gunbelt creaking as he leaned over to take a look.

"This kid. Looks to be at death's door to me."

MUTCH frowned. "She's not haemophiliac is she?"

"Yes. How did you know?" I said.

HUCK rose with alacrity, striking his head on the roof. MUTCH retreated towards the door and stepped out backwards, missing the step and staggering.

"Sweet Jesus Christ," HUCK said. "How long's she been like this?"

"Weeks. Or is it months?" I said to Mira.

"Months," Mira said. "At least."

"She hasn't an opportunistic infection not associated with an underlying immunosuppressive disease or therapy, has she?" HUCK asked.

"Could have," I said.

"Kaposi's sarcoma?"

"Who knows?"

"Chronic generalised lymphadenopathy, unexplained weight loss and/or prolonged unexplained fever?"

39

"Sounds familiar."

"For fuck's sake," HUCK said in a strangled gasp. He followed his colleague and they stood side by side sweating on the hard shoulder. I went to the door and they took a step back together.

"Anything the matter, officers?"

"Your daughter has AIDS," HUCK and MUTCH said in unison.

"First or hearing?"

HUCK and MUTCH glanced at one another as if I were a loonie. I beamed at them. "Is it catching?" I went down a step and they backed away. They kept on backing, identical blank mirrored eyes locked on me, opened the doors of their car and slid inside and wound up the windows.

What a wonderful anti-law device! Poor HUCK and MUTCH! They truly believed they were in danger of catching something nasty from a social status group C2DE, which was what we clearly were, judging by our accents, clothes and the vehicle we drove. Probably zoom straight to HQ, strip, scrub themselves raw under the shower and burn their uniforms. Poor saps!

(It didn't strike me at the time that they might be right: I was too euphoric, having outsmarted them.)

Next stop Sandbach (Road Chef). I adopted the same procedure as before and parked on the edge of the perimeter. Mira said, "Can you get Bev a drink of some kind? I don't want to move her."

"What are you doing?"

"I'll stay here."

"With him?"

"Why not?"

"I'm harmless enough," said Urban Brown with a snide grin.

(Not so long ago you couldn't get the bastard to grin for love nor money; now you couldn't stop him,—all the time grin-grin-grin.)

I stepped over bodies lying in the entrance hall with their sleeping bags, primus stoves and bundles of possessions and joined the single line of people filing upstairs to the first-floor cafeteria, necessitated by the stairway having been taken over for living, eating and sleeping purposes until only a narrow central channel remained for the passage of those using the stat for legitimate reasons. Why, I wondered, didn't the authorities do something? Kick the buggers out. Fine them for public obstruction under Code 11. They'd no right to be here. I hadn't paid any taxes in years but I still felt affronted. What was the country coming to?

The Cafeteria wasn't much better, even though the strays and slags had been disbarred entry, because here the queue stretched right round the room and tailed off outside the door in a disgruntled spiral. A cup of coffee could take two hours of your time minimum. What to do? Bev was burning up and needing liquid, poor sod, but there was no way I was going to become one of the waiting undead.

I pushed and squirmed until I got to the lavatory and held my breath at the acrid stink of standing urine. The drain holes were blocked with fag ends or the flushing system wasn't working or something, and the yellow steaming liquid sloshed brim-full in the stainless steel troughs. I took my shirt off, leaving my white T-shirt on, and rinsed my face and neck, keeping my shirt jammed between my knees so that it wouldn't get stolen. I shimmied across to the towel machine and wiped my hands on the wet bedraggled tail of towel hanging to the floor. This gave me an idea. I wadded my shirt into a tight sausage and wedged it into a back pocket of my jeans. I opened the broken lid of the towel machine, removed the towel on its metal spindle, and wound up the flapping tail. I put the towel on my shoulder and strode purposively into the swarming corridor, calling out the usual phrases such as, "Mind your back! Out we go! Down and at 'em! To your left! Easy over! Up your arse!" and the one that seemed to work best of all, "BACK PASSAGE!!!"—parting them like the Red Sea as I sailed blithely through and into the kitchen unscathed. The cooks and servers in their soiled white hats were too busy to take any notice and I kept up the pretence of meaningful activity, cutting a swathe through the kitchen, lithely swaying my hips to avoid perspiring personnel, protruding handles of pans, stuck-out trays of mashed potato and green peas, so on and so forth, all the while sizing up what was where and how best to get it.

Dumping the soggy towel in a corner behind a pile of rubbish cascading from a rubber dustbin, I went straight for a large metal tray and with the same unconscious aplomb began collecting various soft drinks and sundry portable foodstuffs as if to an order from the Almighty Himself, or at the very least the Catering Manager. No one stopped me, glanced in my direction, turned a hair.

Tray full, I hoisted it above my head and renegotiated my gliding smoothly-coordinated way to the door and out.

A pathway appeared as if by magic (a loaded tray held aloft is as good as a security clearance card) and I waltzed along the corridor and down the stairs, nimble as Nureyev, tip-tap-toe.

"What time does the cafeteria close?" an anxious soul asked me, sweat-dried face upturned beseechingly.

"We never close, sir," I told him sternly. "Or madam."

"Thank you so much," came the humble response.

Conjecturing that a tray being carried out to the parking area might be noticed and remarked upon, I scouted round for a cardboard box or similar receptacle. There was plenty of rubbish lying about but it all belonged to somebody. One box filled with boots and shoes would do admirably, and I approached the owner.

"Your empty box for a packet of sweet digestives," I bartered.

"What else have you got?" said the woman greedily, raising herself up to look at my tray of goodies.

"You can have a packet of biscuits *or* a can of Coke. I just want the box. You can keep the shoes."

"I'll have those shortcakes." She tipped the box and emptied it.

The man next to her on the floor, knees drawn up inside a circle of territorially arranged possessions, face the colour of old cheese, said eagerly, "*Two* empty boxes for a packet of biscuits, any kind."

"I don't need two boxes," I said. "This one will do."

"Keep your nose out," the woman warned him. "We've done a deal."

"Fuck off, you old lesbian," the man retorted.

An old woman behind me said, "This coat for that packet of egg sandwiches. The collar's real fur, feel it."

"In this weather?" I said. "I don't need a coat with a real fur collar." I took the box and transferred the food and drink to it.

"Anything else you need?" asked the woman who had done the deal.

I shook my head.

"I have a bracelet. Platinum . . ."

The man said, "You've got yours, ratbag, give somebody else a chance. How about a cashmere scarf?" he said to me, rummaging for the item in question. "Hardly worn, sir. Good as new."

Somebody thrust a pair of tan brogue shoes under my nose. "Two packets of sandwiches and that can of orange squash. Look at them! They're your size."

I struggled to stand up, holding my box protectively under my arm. I could hardly move for the press of bodies. Somebody got hold of my T-shirt and I yanked free.

"All right then, *one* packet of sandwiches and a can of orange."

"I don't want your shoes." I tried to get out and tripped over legs and feet.

"Real platinum . . ."

"Cashmere . . ."

"Hardly worn . . ."

"Get-that-box," said another, younger, harder voice.

Head down I went for the door, the pack after me, stepping on things and people in a mad headlong rush. Somebody got a hand on my box and I kicked backwards with my heel. I collided with some people coming in through the swing doors and there was a general mêlée of confusion: curses, shouts, screams and shocks.

Outside in the sunshine I ran a few paces and then slowed to get my breath back and not attract attention.

Petrol.

I got my hose and two-gallon can and did a casual walkabout on the outskirts of the parking area. A car with DISABLED

43

DRIVER NO HAND SIGNALS in the back window looked promising. If the driver was thalidomide with rudimentary limbs and knobbly stumps for fingers it could mean that his petrol cap was of the press-on non-locking type. So it proved. In went the hose, a quick suck on the end to draw the petrol below the level of the tank, and gravity and the law of fluid displacement did the rest. Easy-peasy. Just as I was removing the hose a thin boy,—a youth I suppose you'd call him,—sidled round the back of the car and stared at me from the corner of his bloodshot eye. He wore a holey yellow T-shirt with the legend NUKE ARGIE SCUM on a mushroom cloud printed across the chest and denims cut down to shorts with frayed bottoms. Grimy bare feet in laceless Adidas training shoes with the stitching coming undone. I clenched my fists to hit him.

"Heading for the Smoke, squire?" he inquired softly. His teeth had never heard of Pepsodent.

"No, Timbuktu."

"Where's that?"

"Just south of Leicester."

"Got a *melyn cribo*?"

This was underground argot for a yellow card. "No, why, do I need one?"

"If you're going to the Smoke you do. No *melyn cribo*, no work."

"I'm not looking for work."

"How about a Resident Alien permit?"

"You sell those too?"

"Anything you need, sunshine."

A Resident Alien permit would be useful. Without one I wouldn't be able to get medical treatment for Bev. Hospitals were strict about who they admitted these days. "How much?"

"What have you got?" The boy or youth motioned with a scrawny undernourished hand that we ought to move away from the car in case the owner lurched up. His forearms, I noticed, were hard and shiny and lumpy with old puncture marks and scar tissue.

44

"Not a lot of anything," I said. "Petrol any good to you?" The boy or youth shook his head. "What then?"

"Wife? Daughter?"

"Both."

"A double-header for a Resident Alien permit while you watch."

"Suck my cock instead," I said.

"Suck mine for a *melyn cribo*."

"It's probably pox-ridden."

"No blood, just a clear discharge. You could rinse your mouth out with petrol after."

I toyed with the idea of battering him senseless and taking everything he had. Dump his body along the motorway somewhere and let the crows have him. Was he too smart to carry the stuff on him?

"I'll do without it," I said. "You'll give them both a dose."

He shrugged. "A guy's gotta live." He grinned with his melyn teeth. "I've got something else you need even more if you're travelling past Watford Gap."

"What's down there?"

"Trouble."

"In the form of,—?"

"You'll see." He pulled out a foil strip enclosing tablets or capsules in individual blisters on which the brand name *Temporal* in tiny letters was overprinted a hundred times. "This does the trick. Take one each an hour before you hit the Gap and you won't feel a thing." He aquaplaned his flat hand up into the air like a jet taking off. "Like sliding on cream."

"What does it do?" The mêlée in the entrance hall had spilled onto the forecourt. People beaten and trampled. Some blood too. Few curdling screams.

"Operates like the fast-forward on a video recorder," the boy or youth said, holding up the foil strip enticingly between thumb and forefinger. "Shrinks time subjectively from two hours into five minutes. On this stuff you could be in London in less than twenty minutes, half-an-hour at most."

"Subjectively."

"Yep."

"Where would I be objectively?"

"Same place, buddy-boy. The Smoke."

I wasn't sure I was following this. I asked, "And how exactly is it going to keep us out of trouble at Watford Gap?"

"You'll go past it like *that*." He snapped his fingers, pitifully frail.

"In no time at all."

"Ri-i-ight! *In no time at all*. You said it."

"I don't . . ." I frowned.

"Never heard of Einstein? Everything is subjectively relative. Five minutes in a dentist's waiting-room seems like three hours. This stuff operates in reverse. If you lived on *Temporal* every day of your life you'd die of old age within a week. You want some, don't you?" he grinned knowingly.

"Not if it's the same deal as before." I put the can of petrol down, which was getting heavy. The sun was low in the sky, striking pointed shadows across the asphalt. A tremor of unease shook me as I thought about the impending curfew. What would it be like to be stopped by the police while flying on *Temporal*? Perhaps they'd be talking to someone who'd already gone.

"I'll make you another proposition," the boy or youth said. "Contact a friend of mine in London called Fully Olbin. He'll ask you to do him a favour. Do the favour in exchange for the *Temporal*."

"Sounds reasonable." I didn't smile. "How do I meet him?"

"You'll meet him, don't worry."

"How will you know I've kept to my side of the bargain?"

"You'll have used the *Temporal*."

"But suppose I change my mind when I get to London?"

"You won't have used the *Temporal*."

"I will if I've used it already."

"You won't have used it if you don't follow through with the favour," the boy or youth said.

"You mean if I do the favour I'll have used the *Temporal* and if I decide not to do the favour I won't have used the *Temporal*."

"Got it in one," he smiled yellowly.

"But the favour follows the *Temporal*," I said, "not the other way round. You give me the *Temporal* now and you won't know whether I follow through with the favour in London till later."

The boy or youth sighed wearily. "Where have you been living? Never heard of Heisenberg?"

"A new Bavarian lager?"

"Cause can precede effect and effect can precede cause at one and the same time. What you do later affects what you do now,—it's all the same."

"Not in my world," I said, shifting feet.

"Sure. Remember what Max Born said: 'I am now convinced that theoretical physics is actual philosophy'."

Two in one day. First a terrorist loonie and now a mad quantum mechanic. Which of us was going off our rocker, the world or me?

"Suppose I say I'm not going to do the favour,—will you still give me the *Temporal*?"

"That all depends on whether you do the favour or not."

"But you won't know till later."

"So that's when I'll decide."

"How can you decide later whether or not to give me the *Temporal* now?"

"Simple. I won't have given it to you if you don't do the favour and I will have given it to you if you have."

"You call that simple?"

"Is to me, squire."

"All right." I'd made up my mind. "Give me the *Temporal* and I'll do you the favour, how's that? Happy?"

"I thought you'd say that," he said, handing me the foil strip. "That's more than I did."

He was gone, but the evidence that the boy or youth existed was in my hand. I had the *Temporal*. What good it would do remained to be seen. And whether or not I would do the favour ditto.

I suspected that Brown had made love to Mira while I had been away but I had no means of corroborating it. At one time I might have got angry and flown into a jealous rage but now it hardly seemed worth the effort. And I could have been wrong. I didn't want to appear foolish by accusing her of something she hadn't done.

By the time darkness came on we had passed Keele (Trusthouse Forte) and Hilton Park (Rank) and weren't far from Corley (Trusthouse Forte) when the tedious petrol problem was upon us once again.

To fill the mindless hours of driving, with my foot jammed hard against the accelerator, I used to imagine that Shakespeare was sitting next to me and I had the double pleasure of listening to his comments on this (to him) bizarre modern world and explaining to him such mysteries as the square iron boxes which apparently moved of their own volition but were actually powered by Engines burning a refined derivative of crude oil and the principle on which the steady baffling unflickering glow of the motorway lights on their fabricated steel stalks operated.

He marvelled at the smoothness of the carriageways and the ultra neatness of everything. He could understand the signs with their arrows, numbers and other graphic symbols (though not the sign for the disabled, which he took to be a man sitting on a boulder) and after a little initial difficulty was able to read the place-names in their brutal modern script. Being a genius, much of it came as no real surprise to him, though what did surprise him was that while the external world had altered so drastically, being filled with unblemished concrete and moving iron boxes and unflickering illumination, human beings had hardly changed one whit: in fact physically they were exactly the same. He would have conjectured, he told me, that they would have advanced to keep pace with scientific progress, and almost expected to see forms of mutation such as puny hairless bodies and huge swollen brains. And what totally amazed him was when I explained that most people living today hadn't the faintest notion of how the modern world functioned. They had heard at school and through the media about scientific achievements and discoveries, and they used mechanical contrivances every day of their lives, yet few of them knew what these achievements and discoveries meant or of their importance, nor how the machines they depended on worked. As Shakespeare pointed out, most of them had the physical, mental and emotional attributes of people living in his own time. Indeed they might as well have been living in the Middle Ages,—preferably so,—because they were still several hundred years behind the times.

I found these comments and conclusions interesting and spent many a pleasurable hour listening to them, interspersed with my attempting to answer his questions in terms an Elizabethan would understand. The dashboard, I remember, its coloured gauges and vibrating needles in illuminated dials, especially fascinated him. I had the devil's own job trying to explain what stored electricity was.

At Corley a large curved screen dominated the car park on which a free non-stop programme of pop music, news headlines, commercials and soft porn was displayed. When we arrived in darkness they were showing a Selina Southorn quickie, which featured Selina in gymslip and stocking-tops being chastised by a middle-aged schoolmaster in gown and mortar-board, who spanked her bare bottom with a flat ruler. *Thwack! Thwack! Thwack!* It was fairly mild, because it was illegal to show an erect penis in a public place. For that you had to go into a video booth and put a £1 coin in the machine.

"How's Bev?" I asked Mira. I was feeling pretty knackered: I had a sultry thumping headache and my right leg was completely dead. It took me a minute or two to manoeuvre myself out of the seat and into the back.

"Urb thinks she has radiation sickness. Either that or toxic waste poisoning."

"Who?"

"Bev. You just asked me about her."

"No, I meant who thinks that?"

Mira indicated Brown. Urb. They *were* getting on well together.

49

"Are you a doctor?" I said to Brown.

"What do doctors know?" he said with contempt.

"What do *you* know?"

"A lot of things you wouldn't believe."

"I'm in the mood to believe anything," I said irritably. "What makes you think she has radiation sickness or toxic waste poisoning?"

The light from a distant sodium lamp was so feeble that in the darkened interior of the van I could barely make out his humped shadow. Was he was still clutching his precious black bundle?

"It's all part of the plan," Brown answered cryptically.

My pulse quickened. "Do you mean somebody's already dropped the Bomb and they haven't told us about it?"

"Could be."

"I don't think you really know yourself. You're guessing. And what's this about toxic waste?"

"Deliberately dumped."

"Who by?"

The humped shadow moved as he shrugged. "Companies."

"On instructions from the Govt?"

"Possibly."

"Is there a war going on that we haven't been told about?"

"What war?" Mira said. "Who with?"

Brown said, "There's a war going on right here and now. Why do you think the motorways are fenced in?"

It hadn't occurred to me why; they just were.

"Why do you think the police are after me?" he went on.

"Because you're a terrorist," I said.

"You never told me that," Mira said hotly.

I couldn't see, and therefore didn't know, whether she was talking to Brown or me. At any rate, intimate as they might have been behind my back, he hadn't told her everything.

"Spit it out," I said, head throbbing. "Are our children being systematically poisoned or aren't they? And if so, why, and by whom?"

"That and worse," Brown said. "It's an incredible story."

50

"It sounds it."

"I can't see them doing that," Mira said matter-of-factly. "They might be misguided but they're not evil. They're not *Nazis*."

Brown laughed. The only time he ever did. From where I was sitting I could see Selina Southorn's vast naked bottom with symmetrical welts like bloody ski marks on an alpine slope filling the giant screen and reflected on the shiny roofs of several hundred parked cars. The image faded and a commercial replaced it for Lyon's Maid ice cream, fronted by Bob Monkhouse. He made a gesture with both arms outspread and smiled toothingly.

"I can't say any more, it's too dangerous," Brown said.

"You haven't told us *anything*," I protested. "That was the deal, remember? Transport to London in exchange for secrets."

"Yes, but not here." His shadowed bulk was a deeper black than the darkened interior, which was the only indication I had that he was actually there. "I require updated information and if I get it here they'll home in on us. We're too exposed. Nearer Birmingham is safer."

"We're near Birmingham now."

"Not near enough. Once we get to Spaghetti Junction the confluence of motorways will confuse them,—"

(Confluence!)

"—they won't know whether we're heading east on the M6, south on the M5, into the city itself, or the antithesis of all those,—"

(Antithesis!)

"—from there I can contact base in safety and get an update on the situation."

There were a number of questions I wanted to ask. What base and what situation was he referring to? How did he intend to contact this base? He kept using emotive words like "dangerous" and "exposed" and this unsettled me. Again I had the feeling that I had been precluded from knowing certain key facts, that things were going on all around me to which I was oblivious. He spoke of a war, but I knew of no such war, either here or in Urop, or

51

anywhere come to that. He spoke of radiation and toxic waste, neither of which had ever impinged themselves on my consciousness.

About Spaghetti Junction being "safe" he was probably right. This was a serpentine network of several hundred miles of motorway within a very small area which curled in on itself,—up and over other motorways, down and under yet others, winding tighter and tighter until becoming lost before it disappeared Godknows-where in umpteen directions.

Some of the sections had collapsed and finished in mid-air. Contractors still worked on stretches that hadn't been used in twenty years and probably never would be again. Yes, once inside Spaghetti Junction we would be "safe"; nobody could "home in on us" there, whatever that meant.

Bob Monkhouse had been replaced by The Pox, a revolutionary punk rock band (Bev thought they were "crisp") miming to their latest hit *Fire the Schools*, a scorching indictment of the educational system and the way it had betrayed the rising generation. Having been banned by the BBC the record had sold over half-a-million copies, and it was rumoured that a book, stage show and possibly a film based on the lyrics were in the offing. There had been calls from certain quarters not to allow the group back into the country after a recent tour abroad, but as they were UK citizens this was ruled legally out of the question, quite apart, of course, from the matter of their dollar earnings, said to be in seven figures.

"Bev's suppurating," Mira said wretchedly. "Is there nothing we can do?"

I switched on the dim yellow interior light and took a look at her. The scabs on her neck were leaking glutinous fluid. Her face was puffed and blotchy-red. Her eyes were slitted vents. She was scalding hot and pulsing with fever.

"Do you have anything left you can give her?" I said. "Tablets. Anything."

"What tablets?" Mira snorted.

"I thought the doctor gave you some tablets?"

"She finished those weeks ago, before the sores started erupting. You *know* we haven't any tablets."

I ripped off a corner square of foil and extruded a *Temporal* capsule with my thumb. It was pink and black, torpedo-shaped. There was a half-full can of Coke on the formica folding table which I used to swill the capsule down the constricted red maw of her throat. I wasn't expecting results, and in fact nothing happened. Bev was still with us, palpably here in the airless green van, not becoming transparent or entering another time zone or anything spookily supernatural like that.

Mira asked sharply, "What's that you've given her?"

"Febrile depressant," I said, tucking the foil strip out of sight before she could catch a glimpse of what was written on it.

"*You* haven't any money to buy fancy drugs," Mira said accusingly.

"I've had them for some considerable time," I said. "For use in an emergency." I rummaged for the bottle and took a swig in full view of her. Mira blamed everything on me. True, I had no pride and no self-respect left. Next she would be ranting that I was trying to poison our daughter. Winning with some women, wives especially, is impossible. I thought of giving Bev a slug of whisky for good measure but rejected the notion.

"And you," I said to Brown, "had better start talking, and soon. Free transportation, free food and drink, and so far you haven't spilled a bean." I felt like breaking the bottle and grinding the jagged end into his starved working-class face. Some people invite, positively demand, such treatment. And to think that I'd been scared of the little mangy sewer rat! I had thought him sly, dangerous, ruthless,—and so he was, but in the manner of a cornered rat, lips drawn back in a snarl of fake quivering ferocity.

I was in charge here, I was calling the shots, not some self-styled underground "subversive" snivelling in a dark corner, clutching his bundle as though it were a baby, under the delusion he was God Almighty because he claimed to know a couple of things of which the general populace was ignorant.

After the repeated petrol caper we were off again, the van

moving faster now that the sun had gone down and the air was cooler. I couldn't recall such a hot summer for many a long year. What with talk about "radiation sickness" and "toxic waste poisoning" the suspicion insinuated itself into my mind that the authorities were even tampering with the weather. I could even believe they had flown in experts from America to advise them on optimum temperatures to induce national well-being and generate a mood of dazed benevolence. This year a colonial war perhaps, next year a balmy summer; it was a cute and plausible ploy for universal pacification.

There are no signs for Spaghetti Junction and you won't find it on any map. In a sense it's folklore, but it exists all right, the Sargasso Sea of the motorway system. Except in the Sargasso Sea you're stuck in one spot all the time whereas in Spaghetti Junction you never stop moving even though you're going nowhere; same difference.

Another peculiarity is that you're never sure you're inside it until you actually are: there isn't a boundary or dividing line which allows you to make the definitive statement, "We are now in Spaghetti Junction". For a long while you wonder when you're going to reach it and then discover you have. Rather like walking backwards into a warm quicksand you didn't know was there until it's gripped you by the knees and is tenderly sucking at your waist.

(Incidentally, curfew didn't apply here because for the police to find anybody was next to impossible, therefore it was a safe place to circulate the night away.)

(Coincidentally, the Govt and the local authority were at loggerheads over the precise extent of Spaghetti Junction, were it to be disentangled and laid out in a straight line, for the simple reason that one calculated the distance in miles, the other in kilometres. So the actual length had never been resolved to everyone's satisfaction.)

Bone-weary as I was, I had no alternative but to drive on. I popped a blister and swallowed a capsule dry. Something to suck on.

The headlights picked out a scrawl of apposite graffito someone had chalked on one of the underpasses: *Welcome to the Concrete Bowel*. From this I conjectured that we were indeed inside it, rattling and lurching onwards and inwards at a rate of knots. The lights strung above the motorway flickered faultily; some had gone out altogether, their protective covers hanging agape like plastic jaws. Sloughed-off tyres were strewn across the three lanes and shards of glass sparkled crazily as our headlights sent feeble swathes over the ink-black tarmac.

Most of the other traffic had gone,—except for an occasional black limousine which swept silently past, the faces behind the curved tinted glass lit greenly from below by the subdued glow of instruments in sunken casings. Such personages had urgent expense-account business to attend to in distant parts of the kingdom and couldn't afford not to travel at all hours of the day and night, gliding swiftly and surely towards personal gratification and self-fulfilment. In one of these hermetically-sealed containers, at midnight or thereabouts, I glimpsed the etched hawklike profile of Vince Hill, the popular balladeer and cabaret entertainer.

Silence and darkness behind me in the interior of the van. No *Thank you for the birds that sing* to comfort Bev in her wretched hallucinogenic slumber. I could see no activity in the black slice of mirror and dared not glance over my shoulder for fear of sending us crashing into a steel balustrade or concrete abutment. The three lanes had merged into two. Unlit signs zipped by, fragments of names and numbers smearing themselves across my retina. I had no idea where I was going and, to tell the truth, no longer cared. For all I knew we could have been dropping down a shaft into the centre of the earth. I indulged this illusion for a little while, enjoying the sensation that all was beyond my control and I could sit back with a mad happy smile on my face, knowing that gravity had taken over and it was useless to fight it. The molten core beckoned enticingly, seething fingers of fire reaching up greedily like slow-motion lightning. A hot blast scorched my face, singeing my eyebrows and moustache. I fought for breath. Were we on fire?

Looking to the east I searched for the dawn but the bastard was nowhere to be found.

The dawn never did come. Neither Mira nor Brown commented on the fact, or non-fact, so I reckoned it politic to do the same. Plus I had my hands full driving and my eyes were never still, looking for a sign that said *London* or *The South* or simply ⟶.

(It's always the same, isn't it? Signs galore lead you *into* somewhere but nary a one tells you how to get *out*. It's as if they fiendishly want to keep you there, endlessly circling purgatory with the fuel gauge nudging zero and your bladder fit to burst.)

Brown had made the observation that by entering Spaghetti Junction we would confuse the authorities as to which direction we were taking; what he hadn't said was that it would confuse us also. Maybe we were now travelling towards Bristol, say, instead of London, or back north up the M6, or just going round and round the same endless piece of two-lane tarmacadam. Without landmarks it was impossible to tell.

(And without the dawn equally impossible to know whether we were moving forward in time or repeating the same minute, moment, and therefore ourselves, *ad nauseam*.)

There is a theory that with each passing nano-second another universe splits itself off from our existing universe and takes a new direction in time and space. A nano-second later another universe splits itself off from this second universe into a third, which also takes a new direction; and a nano-second after that the third universe splits itself off and takes yet another, fourth, direction. So on and so on. And each of these separate multiplying universes in turn split themselves off, nano-second by nano-second, into other universes, which continue splitting and separating every nano-second of recorded time. The theory goes that each of these universes inhabits "a state of probability", that each is as likely to exist as any of the others, and that we, as conscious beings, must

56

thread our way through this multifarious labyrinth as we progress from birth to death. Therefore it follows that alongside the universe we perceive with our senses there is an infinite number of other probable universes, none of which is more real than ours, just as ours is no more real than all the others. Further, this hypothesis goes on to state that as each universe splits into the next, we split with it, with the result that an infinite number of our probable selves inhabits an infinite number of probable universes. It occurs to Vail (whose thoughts these are) that if only it were possible to switch tracks, skipping from universe to universe, he might light upon a universe more to his liking. And with this thought comes another: as new universes are still being created, nano-second by nano-second, it follows that,—because his probable self inhabits each of them,—he has an infinite number of choices before him. One probable self will continue driving for evermore on this same endless stretch of motorway, while another will suffer a heart attack and crash into a bridge, while another will stop the van and go for a pee in the bushes, while another will see a sign saying *London: This Way*, while another will hear furtive scuttlings in the back and realise that his wife and Brown are having intercourse, while another will hear a strangled wail as Mira discovers that their child has died, while another will grin with relief at the sight of a stat ahead, its rosy glow on the concrete horizon mimicking the false dawn that thus far has failed to materialise. All these were possibilities (more correctly, probabilities) which he might take in the future. Yet the annoying thing about the theory was that it didn't give one the power to choose. For example, another of his probable selves was at this precise moment sitting down to a hearty meal in a warm, softly-lit restaurant with a piano playing Noel Coward in the background (in an infinite number of probabilities anything and everything is possible) while this probable self, inhabiting this particular world-line, *this* Vail, was still driving hopelessly in the pre-dawn through the Concrete Bowel with wife, child and underground terrorist. Indeed, as he realised, a probable self of his existed somewhere who hadn't been intrigued by Brown's story and had refused to provide him with transportation. Still another of his probable selves in another probable universe hadn't started out on the journey at all and was at this moment standing at the bar of the Albion quaffing whiskies with half pint bitter chasers. Farther back, moreover, another wouldn't have married Mira in the first place, and in consequence was now a millionaire entrepreneur merchandising Selina Southorn video pornlets and at this point in time lying next to her smooth brown body beside a swimming pool in Tenerife. This really was the bloody annoying part: that of all the infinite number of probable universes in existence, I was stuck with this one, and seemingly didn't have the power to choose or switch.

One such probable universe (the one I happened to be inhabiting) now hove into view: a rosy glow on the concrete horizon mimicking the false dawn that thus far had failed to materialise. I grinned with relief at the sight.

The blue and white sign said: *Watford Gap Services.*

Mira broke away from whatever she was doing and raised herself to peer over the folding formica table. Her hair was tousled and her eyelids swollen with fatique. Perhaps, I thought charitably, she actually had been asleep and not having intercourse with Brown behind my back.

"Are we here?"

"Are we where?"

"I don't know. Where are we?"

"Watford Gap."

"We're not in Spaghetti Junction any more?"

"Apparently not."

"Thank God. I'm parched."

"How's Bev?"

"Still in a coma. The fever's gone."

"How's Brown?"

"How should I know?"

58

"He's back there with you."

"He's back here but he's not *with* me. Not in the Biblical sense."

"I didn't mean to imply that he was. It was just a friendly inquiry."

"Well ask him yourself. He's got a tongue in his head."

This conversation having apparently run out of steam, I didn't pursue it.

"Where are we?" Brown said.

"For God's sake, don't you start," I said, setting the handbrake. I sounded irritable but in actual fact I was rather pleased. This being Watford Gap meant we were on the M1, which was something of an achievement. A brief rest, something to eat and drink, petrol, and we could crash straight down to the Smoke in a matter of hours, arriving at dawn, whenever that happened to be. It crossed my mind that the Govt had tampered with that too for some reason,—either postponing it temporarily or extending the night indefinitely. Possible.

I couldn't put my finger on it, but this stat seemed different somehow. One of the reasons might have been that it was quiet, though I supposed that at this time of the night/early hours of the morning there would be few people about anyway. Still, it was exceedingly quiet.

Some of the buildings were in darkness, including the Macdonalds' burger joint. Less than a dozen cars, I counted, were on the car park, and of these four rested on their haunches, minus wheels. Unusually, too, the large curved screen was blank and silent, and the stanchioned speakers which normally poured forth pop music night and day non-stop were empty black mouths murmuring hollowly in the slight movement of air which you could hardly call a breeze.

Brown got out and stretched himself up to his full five-feet-four. He raised his arms alternately, swapping the bundle from armpit to armpit to facilitate this action. I'd made up my mind to leave him here. So far he'd been nothing but a smart-ass pain-in-the-neck, and possibly a wife-fucker into the bargain.

59

Leaving Mira and Bev in the van we approached the main entrance which consisted of five pairs of double glass doors, two of which stood ajar. We entered. The foyer was in semi-darkness. We went up the stairs, following the direction indicated by the arrowed sign saying CAFETERIA. Behind the chest-high glass-and-laminate partition which walled off the cafeteria from the passageway, eight or nine young men were sitting astride huge powerful motorcycles with twin exhausts. The machines were buffed and polished to gleaming perfection. The young men, all of whom I recognised, were wearing black leather, chains and denims, and it was impossible at first glance to see where the bodies of the young men ended and the machines began, as each appeared to merge into the other.

I remember thinking *They must have had prosthetic surgery*, and this was an astute guess on my part as it turned out. I can be pretty smart at times.

"Hey, you guys," I called out. 'Any chance of getting something to eat and drink around here?" I said this in a confident, friendly voice, consciously adopting the indolent stance of their body language and the lackadaisical manner of what I assumed to be their speech patterns.

(Incidentally, I've noticed this trait in others as well as in myself: that of genuflecting to certain people in similar fashion to those apes which present their backsides and balls to a potential adversary as a gesture of prior submission.)

"If you were hoping to score you can butt out," James Dean said, swivelling round from the hips to address me. "We're users, not pushers."

"No, no, you got me wrong," I said. "We want food and drink, not dope. Anything at all will do."

"Who is this turkey?" asked Marlon Brando.

Elvis Presley, Gene Vincent and Eddie Cochran shrugged their shoulders. Sal Mineo sneered a little. Jerry Lee Lewis ran a comb through his long wavy hair and said, "You got permission to invade our turf?"

"It was open so we just came on in," I said. "No offence."

"Who is you guys?" asked Little Richard. He was astride a Harley-Davidson with low-slung handlebars and a quilted backrest. The plastic job on his face hadn't taken as well as the others; the cheekbones weren't quite right and the dark skin tone was patchy. The pencil moustache looked good though.

I introduced myself and Urban Brown. "We're not here to cause any trouble. We just stopped by for something to eat."

"Trouble?" Marlon grunted, raising a sardonic eyebrow above a hairy throat. "I hear you mention trouble, boy?"

Brown whispered in my ear: he didn't like the look of the situation: he wanted out.

"Don't WHISPER!" Gene yelled, leaning forward over the tank and pointing his black gloved finger straight at us like the barrel of a gun. His curly hair was stuck with perspiration to his forehead. There was a kinda glazed look in his eyes.

"We'd better just split," I suggested, turning towards the stairs, but Jimmy said no, come on through, so we did. Close to I could see that the fuel lines went into the femoral arteries on the insides of their thighs and that their shinbones were grafted onto the metal footrests. Part of the bikes' electric starter system was incorporated into their left wrists: switches, knobs and dials. Neat.

"Where ya truckin', white trash?" Elvis asked with his famous lopsided leer.

I was about to answer and thought better of it. I said, "Frisco."

"Faggotsville," said Eddie with a lazy grin. "Jeez, we ain't terrorised that burg in a long whiles."

So far Buddy Holly hadn't said anything. He had the stereo speakers attached to his rear forks turned low and was nodding and clicking his fingers to *Twenty Flight Rock*.

"Any chicks with you?" Jerry Lee said, flicking the grease out of his comb.

I shook my head. "Uh-huh."

"Dope?" (Gene)

"Nope."

"Gas?" (Jimmy)

"Sorry," I said. "Fresh out."

61

"What kinda wheels you got?" Sal asked me.

"Truck. Er, pick-up. Station wagon."

"Well which for goddamn fucksakes!"

"Sort of a covered pick-up."

"What's in the bundle?" Jimmy asked, running his fingers through his shock of hair.

"Radio equipment."

"You a ham?" Eddie said to Brown, who nodded his matted head.

"Looks more like a bum to me," Marlon said. There were grins, leers and smirks all round.

"I vote we bounce these dudes round the parking lot," said Little Richard with a brilliant manic smile. "We're due for some fun. What say?"

With a twist of his left wrist Elvis gunned his machine into throaty life. Choking blue smoke swirled everywhere. I coughed and stepped back, covering my mouth. Brown retreated to the wall. Elvis blipped the throttle and the noise nearly lifted the roof off. Marlon waved his hand and Elvis cut the revs to an idling rumble. "We'll check out their wheels first," Marlon said. He shrugged his ponderous shoulders. "Never can tell, they might have something stashed away. Booze, dope, chicks, gas." He jerked his thumb at me as an indication that we should precede them outside. When the rest of the pack started up you could hardly hear yourself think. In seconds the place was filled with thick blue fog. I lost sight of Brown and was barely able to grope my way to the stairs. My throat was burning and my lungs had seized up.

The machines followed us down the stairs and out onto the pitted and rubbish-strewn concrete of the car park. I now knew why the stat was abandoned and deserted. This mob of prosthetic-implanted look-alikes had taken over Watford Gap and held sway over twenty or thirty miles of motorway. And what, I fumed, were the authorities doing about it? Bugger all.

I leapt aside as Gene aimed the blazing headlamp of his Triumph Bonneville straight at me, his rawboned face and bulging brown eyes alive with drug-crazed glee. The pack had turned on their stereo systems and we were assailed by a rock 'n' roll cacophony of horrendous proportions.

Sal swerved into Brown and pried his bundle loose. He rode off with it with a whoop and a holler, holding the prize above his head. Headlights zig-zagged back and forth, crossed and criss-crossed each other. The booming roar of engines obliterated the night.

Marlon and Eddie and Jerry Lee were over by the van. I ran across with Brown scuttling crab-wise behind me, in time to see Eddie open the side door and stick his blond quiff inside. Jerry Lee held up a warning gloved hand and I slowed to a trot and stopped a few feet away. The others rode up and hemmed us in with idling machinery. Brown looked despairingly at the bundle in Sal's grasp.

"It's a no-no," Eddie said, ducking back out and shaking his head.

"Zilch?" Marlon said, disbelief and disappointment in equal measure on his broad heavy features. He turned to me glower-ingly. "What gives?"

I assumed what I thought was a reasonably creditable ex-pression of innocence and said, "Like I told you. Zeroesville. My buddy and me were just passing through, heading for Frisco. We don't have a red cent between us."

"Listen, meathead," Marlon snarled. "This is our ground and we don't take kindly to goddamn fucking spics and wetbacks crashing in without paying their dues."

"Easy on that," Sal said, stiffening.

"Present company excepted," Marlon said, his attention still fixed on me. "We want. What you got?"

I took the strip of *Temporal* from my back pocket and handed it over.

"You can have this. It isn't much good. I tried it and nothing happened. But feel free."

"You lying crud!" Gene exploded. "You had a fix all along and you held out!"

Before I knew what was happening he lashed out and the

63

sharpened studs on his jacket sleeve gouged chunks from my cheek and neck.

"Okay, okay," Marlon soothed him. "Don't get uptight. Now we've got the stuff we can take care of them in our own sweet time."

Brown said, rather foolishly I thought, "Cut the crap you punks and let me have my bundle back." (At least he was getting the hang of the jargon.) "If you don't you might live to regret it."

"Sez who?" Elvis said, and aimed a vicious karate chop at Brown, ineffectual as it happened, because Brown was out of reach.

"Nobody takes this from me," Sal said, clutching the bundle. "Nobody."

"All right," said Brown, "if that's how you want to play it," and seemed to lose all further interest in the proceedings.

I was still busy sopping up blood from my face and neck. The pain should start any second now, I reckoned. The cuts were good and deep.

"I'm getting bored, let's finish it," Buddy complained, and for the first time I noticed another mistake: his thick black-framed glasses weren't real but painted onto his head like Groucho's moustache.

Jimmy yawned. "He's right. Let's wishbone the creeps."

"Wishbone?" I glanced round vaguely.

"Where ya bin living?" Eddie said, and suddenly grinned like a lighthouse beam. "Never heard of wishboning?" He guffawed.

Everybody was smiling and nodding now,—even Marlon. The atmosphere was quite jolly. I said, "No, never have," and grinned too to show that I was a good sport, could take a joke with the best of them.

"What we do," Gene confided, watery brown eyes alight, "is we wrap a chain around your left leg and a chain around your right leg. Following me so far? We fasten one of the chains to his bike and the other chain to my bike. Then Eddie and me, we say 'So long', and we go our separate ways. Me this way, him that way. Get it? And you come with the both of us. Some of you comes with me and some of you with him. If you get my drift. Then we decide the winner."

"What winner?"

"Whoever's got the biggest piece. Why you think it's called 'wishboning', schmuck? You mentally retarded or somethin'?"

I found it hard to believe that they really intended to do this. What was the point? We'd given them all we had to give, which was precious little, admittedly. Was this how they got their "kicks", by murdering innocent people? I looked helplessly at Brown, but he was staring off into space, or rather into the surrounding darkness beyond the halo of light, as if none of this concerned him. I wrung the blood out of my handkerchief and swabbed some more.

Then Little Richard had a wonderful idea. As a preamble to the main event, how about setting fire to the van and watching her blow? Jimmy, both arms draped over the handlebars, fingers loosely spread, gave a twitch of a shrug, which was his way of expressing approval. Elvis leered his, while Gene's perspiring face lit up, and Eddie growled, "Right on."

Buddy was clicking away to *Blue Jean Baby*, Jerry Lee combing his locks, and Sal muttering darkly about guys who let their mouths run away with them shouldn't be surprised to find a spic knife between their shoulderblades one dark night. Marlon said, "Like it. Let's do it," and thus it was decided.

Watching the interior of the van brighten and flicker with flame, I couldn't help thinking of Mira and Bev in the long drawer underneath the bunk, which was where they had presumably concealed themselves when Eddie poked his head inside and found it empty.

No good worrying about that now, I told myself, as the fire reached the petrol tank and the van erupted in a spectacular orange fireball, buffeting our faces with a solid wall of heat even at a distance of thirty metres or so. I wrung out my sticky hand-kerchief.

Brown sidled up and said out of the corner of his mouth, "What was the registration number?"

I shook my head. "Won't do any good. It wasn't insured. Besides, the MOT had run out."

"The number," he said through clenched lips. "And lie flat."

I failed to see the connection between these two disparate requests. Still he stared at me. It took a moment or two to remember what it was. "FTJ 109V," I said.

"Thank you," Brown said, kicking my legs from under me.

He was crouching and fiddling with a small square black device with a short retractable antenna, and the next thing I knew there was a flash of light and a blast that nearly ruptured my eardrums and pieces of hot oily metal were showering down all around us. When I dared to look over the crook of my elbow there was a respectable crater where the pack, moments before, had been clustered; all that remained was a smoking junkyard and the odd twitching dismembered carcase.

"I told them to give it back," Brown said, levering himself up. "They can't say I didn't warn them."

"I thought it was a radio," I said.

"A radio with four pounds of gelignite inside it. Triggered by shortwave." He put the device back in his pocket. "They really ought to have listened. I did warn them."

"You did," I agreed, getting up and dusting myself down. "They can't say you didn't."

"They can't say anything now," Brown said, giving me an impish sidelong glance. This was the one and only humorous remark I ever heard him utter.

"Why did you want to know the registration number?"

"I used it as the DFC."

I raised, then lowered my eyebrows.

"Detonating Frequency Code. Then like a fool forgot it. Lucky you remembered."

"Lucky's not the word," I said.

"What is then?"

"What is what?"

"The word."

"What word?"

"The word other than lucky."

"What other word other than lucky?"

"You said 'Lucky's not the word'. I'm asking you what is."

"No idea."

"Then why say lucky wasn't the word if it was?"

"It's an expression, 'Lucky's not the word'. It doesn't mean there *is* another word. It's a figure of speech."

"I've never heard it."

"Take my word for it."

"What word?"

"My word. My assurance."

"'Assurance' is the word then?"

"Look," I said. "Let's just say it was lucky I remembered. Will that do?"

"Fine by me."

"Swell."

This futile conversation had distracted me from the van, all ablaze. As we approached it the molten core beckoned enticingly, seething fingers of fire reaching up greedily like slow-motion lightning. A hot blast scorched my face, singeing my eyebrows and moustache. I fought for breath.

We were on fire!

We had stopped, slewed slantwise on the hard shoulder. I scrambled out and ran round to the side door, wrenched it open and dived inside, hands outstretched in the dark to where I knew the fire extinguisher to be. It was there all right, but it was rusted into its bracket.

Mira screamed to know what was happening. I was out of breath with panic and exertion and couldn't answer her. Fumes filled the interior.

"Why are we on fire?" Brown asked, which struck me as rather an irrelevant question under the circumstances.

The engine hissed and spat as I smothered it with foam. It

seemed positively angry about something, as if I had foiled its carefully-planned attempt at suicide. Engines can be such bad-tempered buggers. All along it had carried us grudgingly, just waiting for a chance to explode, and had chosen its moment well,—here in the dead-end of nowhere,—leaving me to cope with a sick child, an irascible wife and a terrorist loonie.

I was so embittered I hadn't the patience or the inclination to answer Shakespeare's questions and told him to piss off; let him find out about the trials and tribulations of the modern world from somebody else for a change.

Inside Brown's bundle (you might have guessed) was a radio transceiver.

He set it up behind some dusty bushes just off the hard shoulder and twiddled some knobs. There were a couple of squawks and a tinny voice spoke in a foreign accent. Brown asked questions about the "current situation" and requested an "update", the answers to which I didn't understand, though apparently Brown did. Could we summon help? I asked Brown; no, we couldn't. The authorities might be eavesdropping and if we mentioned our location over the airwaves (where *was* our location?) they would have not the slightest trouble in sending a squad to "take us out".

"But that's what I want," I said. "To be taken out."

Brown shook his starved rat's face impatiently. To "take us out", he explained, was a euphemism for death by slaughter. We would be machine-gunned and left to decompose in the bushes. I replied that I found this somewhat fanciful, if not downright melodramatic.

More unintelligible gabble came over the set and I thought I caught a reference to "Libyan logistical support" which, I noticed, made Brown suck at his teeth excitedly. Was this, then, an international conspiracy? Who was banding together with whom, and for what purpose? In my mind's eye I visualised the entire country alive with secret subversive cells, a grid or network of political plotters and social disrupters from coast to coast. Why were they never mentioned on any TV newscast? Why didn't the *Sun* do an in-depth analytical exposé on them?

It seemed incredible to me that all this underground activity was going on and nobody knew anything about it. At home on Zuttor Estate we were kept in ignorance of such matters. They might have been taking place on another planet.

Brown retracted his antenna, switched off the set and wrapped it away in his thick black overcoat. He appeared mordantly pleased. His ravaged face creased in a grin. "Didn't believe me, eh? You heard it for yourself: the big one is about to blow!"

"The only thing I heard was a garbled reference to 'Libyan logistical support'. Are they part of your outfit?"

"Them and the INLA," Brown said. "And the Red Brigade and Black September."

These sounded to me, respectively, like the French national railway system and two heavy metal rock bands, but I didn't betray my ignorance. Instead I asked, "What's this big one that's about to blow?"

"Dungeness B."

"What's that?"

"A fast-breeder gas-cooled reactor."

"A nuclear power station?" When he nodded alertly, eyes alive in his thin drab face, I said, "That's going to cause a bit of a mess, isn't it? Won't it lay waste to large areas of the countryside?"

"Towns and people too. You can say goodbye to Sussex and Kent for a start. If the wind's in the right direction London might cop it."

I had never seen him so vibrant. He was positively brimming. It seemed to me that he didn't so much want to change the social order as destroy it altogether. He was motivated not by reforming zeal but by petty infantile spite. Either something horrible had happened to him in childhood, I surmised, or he had been born with a meanness of spirit, one of the world's natural runts or recklings. Given wealth, power and prestige (and he would have to be given them, he could never have achieved them by his own

69

efforts) he would have lorded it over the rest of us in the manner of the most aloof and disdainfully overbearing aristocrat imaginable.

"I don't like the sound of that," Mira said, cradling Bev in her arms. "That's where we're going. Hardly fair on us to wipe it out before we get there. Selfish if you ask me."

Brown made a motion of the shoulders. "It's all to the good in the long term," he said. "We can't pick and choose who gets it in the neck and who doesn't. Personally I think wholesale carnage is the only way to bring them to their senses."

"That's all very well for you to say," Mira expostulated, rocking Bev. "What happens to our sick child? The whole purpose of this journey is to seek proper medical attention and you have the nerve to inform us there won't be a doctor left standing when we get there! Is this a sample of the 'new social order' you keep rabbiting on about? Well, I'll tell you, I don't think much of it!"

"We didn't start the war, they did," Brown said placidly. "We didn't dump toxic chemicals adjacent to urban populations. It wasn't us who turned a blind eye to environmental pollution and let the chemical companies get away with murder. We weren't instrumental in allowing canisters of radioactive waste to be buried next to schools and council estates. Neither did we instigate the series of medical experiments on the children of the poor. Don't lay these anomalies at our door. Lay them fair and square where they belong. You can't blame your child's condition on us."

"Wait a minute," I said, frowning. "If what you say is true, and all this is going on, I have two questions. One: what is the purpose, the objective, of this toxic and radioactive waste dumping policy or programme, and, two: how and why is what you're doing any different?"

The answers sprang instantly to Brown's lips. "The objective is to reduce unnecessary and unproductive urban population, and what we're doing is different in intent but not in kind."

"You admit then that you also want to decimate large numbers of the population," I said. A thin chill wind from nowhere rattled the leaves of the bushes. There were few operating lights on this section of motorway, which cast the embankment, a bridge farther along, and our crouching figures into murky gloom: these were the dead hours between two a.m. and the first rays of the false dawn.

"We don't *want* to," Brown said. "We *have* to. In this day and age shock tactics are the only ones that work. Killing soldiers doesn't grab the headlines any more. Killing horses grabs a few but you can't go on killing livestock without alienating the animal-loving public, which in the long term is counter-productive. Our strategy has been meticulously planned and coordinated at the highest level by people who know what they're about."

"Who are these people?" I interrupted. "Are you prepared to give us their names?"

"I would if I could but I can't."

"You're not high up enough in the echelon to know?" I suggested mischievously. But this didn't have the desired effect, and he answered non-committally:

"Have it your own way," and added, "In any case, the names of the people at the top aren't important. Their identities are known to a very few. We serve an ideology, not personalities."

"How do you know they're not leading you astray?"

"Because the authorities have proscribed our activities and would do anything to get their hands on us. We and our sister organisations are a thorn in their side. There wouldn't be a ten thousand pound reward out for information leading to our apprehension if we weren't a threat to public order and governmental stability."

"Ten thousand pounds," Mira said in a voice of quiet awe, and from the position of her head I could tell she was looking at me and not at Brown.

I said, "That's a pretty good amount these days, even in dollars. It would tempt most people if not everybody."

"Temptation's one thing," said Brown.

"What's the other?"

"What?"

"The other thing."

"What other thing?"

"You said 'Temptation's one thing'. When people say that they qualify it by saying 'and something-else-or-other is another'."

"What something else?"

"I don't know. It was your thought, not mine. I don't know what else you were going to say."

"I wasn't going to say anything else."

"Just 'Temptation's one thing' and leave it at that?"

"Yes."

"In that case it doesn't make sense. 'Temptation's one thing', on its own doesn't mean anything."

"Perhaps it doesn't to you."

"To anybody," I said. "What does it mean to you?" I asked Mira.

"What? I wasn't listening," Mira said. "I'm cold. Can we go back in the van? Have we anything to eat, I'm starving."

"How's Bev?" I said, realising I was cold too.

"She appears to be in some sort of coma," Mira said, struggling to get up. I helped her to her feet. Where was Bev in her head? I wondered. In London? Still back at the Sandbach stat? Or somewhere else? I still wasn't clear in my own mind how *Temporal* worked. Presumably it displaced or telescoped time in some way,—subjectively, that's to say, as the boy or youth had said. The body moved through time in the normal way while the brain, or rather the mind, inhabited a different set of spatial coordinates. Mind you, I hadn't noticed anything untoward after taking it.

Wherever Bev was, I hoped she wasn't suffering.

"What do you think, is it safe to leave here?" I said to Brown when we were inside the van. It was still very dark, the four of us merely shapes without substance.

"The point is, *can* we leave here?" Brown said. "Will the van start or won't it? If the engine's kaput, then we can't."

On the face of it this was a true statement, and in fact made far more sense than his previous "Temptation's one thing" nonsense. Of course he was right in the respect that temptation *was* one thing (as distinct from two), but where did that get us? Not very fucking far.

72

It reminded me,—why I don't know,—that for years and years I had gone around thinking that the word "varmint" was spelt "varmit". I pronounced it as "varmit" too, and can still recall the shock of incredulity when the error was pointed out to me. At first I refused to concede that I was wrong, yet there it was in the dictionary's cold print, plain as a pikestaff. It was a most disorientating experience which for a while threw the entire fabric of existence askew, and one I wouldn't wish to repeat for all the tea in Ceylon.

However: this reminiscence, fascinating as it was, didn't help in getting us off the hard shoulder. Would the engine start or wouldn't it,—that was the question.

The deserted motorway in the thick of night offered no salvation. Nine times out of ten anything that did by chance happen to come along would be a sleek black bullet-proof limo en route from one exotic location to the next, the serried faces inside frozen into immobile tight-lipped greenish masks of somnambulance . . .

"What's that!" Brown said abruptly.

"What!" I said, startled half out of my wits.

"Nothing."

"What was it?"

"I thought I heard something."

All three of us listened. I could hear nothing.

"What did it sound like?"

"I'm not sure."

"Look!" Mira whispered.

A pillar of light was moving towards us along the central reservation. With it come the sound of enormous wings beating the air in rhythmic surges.

—*whoosh!*

      —*whoosh!*

           —*whoosh!*

                —*whoosh!*

                    —*whoosh!*

The searchlight from the sky (for such it was) of several million candlepower kept to a steady track, throwing a perfect blinding disc onto the tarnished and slipstreamed grass which sort of grew between the corrugated crash barriers. The *whooshing* increased in volume and intensity until the metal clips securing the van's interior light fitment reverberated in sympathy. How high the helicopter was it was impossible to gauge because there was no point of reference except the solid dark air, which was none at all; it might have been twenty metres or two hundred.

"They couldn't have traced it," Brown mumbled. "They couldn't."

"Here's your chance to add more scalps to your already impressive total," I said, relishing his fear. "Knock them out of the sky and get a bagful in one fell swoop. You could be an underground hero!"

The air pressure rocked the van on its springs.

"What will they do?" Mira said, almost having to scream it as the threshing of enormous blades came practically overhead.

"According to your friend Urb here, machine-gun us without compunction," I yelled back. "Splatter us to smithereens and leave what's left to the carrion." I wasn't acting brave; for some strange reason I wasn't afraid, which confused me.

The light moved past our windows, neither deviating to left or right, throwing out a brilliant reflected afterglare which transformed the interior of the van into daytime.

Brown's face changed as I watched it, realising that the helicopter wasn't searching for us and hadn't seen us, continuing on its chosen path towards the bridge about three hundred and fifty metres away. The air still beat in our ears, just as the column of light was scorched onto our eyeballs, renewed with each blink so that the imprinted image kept interfering with the real one, now a silvery pencil diminishing in the direction in which the van was pointing.

Threads came from above and down these threads slid figures clad in black from head to toe. They swung onto the parapet of the bridge and swarmed over it like lice. The beam of light went out and the helicopter moved off until it was a distant throb.

74

"All that performance surely isn't for us," Mira said, rather awed and bemused.

"Anti-insurgence squad on manoeuvres," said Brown knowledgeably, having regained his starving rat composure. "In case they have to quell a riot, storm an embassy or rescue a pop star. In their spare time," he added, "they rob mail trains."

"Why should they do that?" I inquired.

"Boost battalion funds. It helps pay for booze-ups, stag shows and day trips."

"They're not after us then?"

I couldn't see his shake of the head in the darkened interior but assumed he had. I almost wished they *had* come for us: it could have meant ten thousand smackeroos for Brown's capture, as well as rescuing us from the Concrete Bowel, which apparently led to the arse-end of nowhere.

To my surprise it seemed that the fire had taught the engine a lesson, because for all its sulky recalcitrance the varmint started at once, and we lurched onto the inside lane and picked up speed to achieve a respectable 25 mph.

As I drove I wondered about the mood that lay over sleeping England this night. To tell the truth, I couldn't fathom it. Could anyone?

Another England slumbered in my consciousness, in my green memory.

A quiet country road. Sunlight dappling the hedgerows. Hovis for Tea. Bulky policemen on creaking bicycles. A whitewashed pub with a curl of blue smoke coming from the chimney (quaint!). The dozing drone of a Spitfire on recce patrol. A sign saying S-Bend Ahead. Or better still, Hump-Backed Bridge. Fields cut and stacked with golden cubes. A train belching sparks emerging from a tunnel. A cream-and-blue single-decker bus with big headlamps labouring up a hill. A tiny red bull-nosed Post Office van with parcels inside fastened with thick string and blobs of sealing-wax. A prospect of hills like soft green breasts. A woman wearing a tweed skirt and sensible shoes buying cauliflower and a pound of tea in a village store. The tip of a church spire gleaming goldenly in the setting sun. The sound of fat car tyres on crunchy gravel. A schoolboy with an S-shaped snake belt and woollen stockings collapsed about his ankles. Two old men with pipes and a basking dog sitting on a bench outside a pub.

—This was the probable universe I inhabited in my dream of dreams. A pleasant slumbering languorous landscape. Such a world I had experienced as a child, not directly, but in the yellowing pages of old periodicals, themselves redolent of hot dusty summers and damp autumns lush with decay. In this other, mythical England, before my time, more real to me than my own childhood, shock-haired children with pale spindly necks and jutting sandy knees busied themselves on beaches with buckets and spades. The boys had braces strung over their skinny shoulders, rib cages exposed like fossil remains, supporting an excessive volume of thick grey flannel on their lean shanks; the girls with freckled noses and straight lank hair tucked their flapping print dresses into blue knickers and scampered about between the sandcastles, legs flashing like thin blades. Not far away, across the tramlines on the promenade, the saloon bars seethed with romantic liaisons, betting tips and boisterous holiday spirit. Warm dark beer frothed from pumps and the ceiling writhed with nicotine. The young men, in smart V-necked pullovers and open-necked shirts, stood back on their heels at the bar and surveyed the world with confident masculine disdain, in between opinions casting their eyes about for the pretty young woman but not overly concerned because tonight on the dance-floor beneath the mirror-faceted globe and spinning flecks of light was the proper time for that, while here and now was for serious drinking and worldly debate, unless, of course, a fast tart happened by.

In this memory I took no part. I was the omnipresent onlooker, the fascinated bystander, soaking up the atmosphere, senses all aquiver for sentient data, the memory made flesh.

From the calorific seaside I swung my inner eye to a damp mossy churchyard under the dripping elms and a bird of some kind perched on a twig. Slanting rain emptied steadily from the skies,

76

drowning the world in grey mist. A leering gargoyled spout gurgled and spewed clear cold rainwater into a stone trough, its incessant insane chuckle making the silence more oppressive. There, not far away, on the flanks of the hillside, stood a horse with head bowed at one end, bedraggled tail at the other. No figures moved in this grey vision; it was a sodden England under a perpetual downpour, drinking its fill, the thrust of growth checked and in abeyance until the watery sun broke through and burned off the excess of moisture in the saturated fields and in the narrow puddles formed by the rutted tracks. Long meandering walls of dark stone gleamed damply in the drab light, reaching away into the obscure distance.

Another page turned, another vision beckoned, this time of smart people with groomed heads smoking du Maurier cigarettes, long delicate fingers dangling negligently over the sides of wicker chairs, grave seamless faces turned towards the camera as they prepared to fly the Clipper across the Atlantic. In the background hovered an anonymous white-coated attendant holding a silver tray, his bland closed expression apeing those of his masters and betters grouped around the glass-topped table. The gentlemen wore evening dress, the ladies gowns of clinging silken stuff which followed every line and crevice of their slender breastless bodies, for dinner above the clouds was a sumptuous solid silver affair. Their careless ease spoke of apartments in Mayfair and Bentley tourers and weekends in the country where they tramped the Downs in stout shoes and herring-bone capes, calling the setters to heel and debating the League of Nations.

In contrast another image shunted into view, one of clamorous activity and swirling smoke beneath the ribbed and strutted vault of a large railway station. Carriage doors stood open, worn leather straps handing down, the carriages identified by their livery and ornate gold initials. Pungent steam drifted over the tracks, crept onto the platforms and sidled through the iron spokes of bogeys lined up in convoy and laden high with severe square parcels and grey sacks and shapeless brown paper packages. The giant arrowed hands of a moon-faced clock jerked the seconds away, a whistle sounded, doors crashed, a flag waved, and the grinding acceleration began to gather momentum with squealing wheels and explosive gusts of expended energy. Through the smoke the legends of a lost civilization shifted and fragmented, appeared and faded in mocking farewell: Craven 'A', Borwick's Baking Powder, Nugget Polish, Colman's Starch, Dr Scholl Zino-Pads, Mackeson's Milk Stout, Bear Brand Pure Silk Stockings, Phosferine Tonic, Bovril Puts Beef Into You, Silvo Liquid Silver Polish, Wills's Whiffs.

Memory was fallacious of course. This England never existed, except in back numbers of *National Geographic*. Long, long before Europe became Urop. Yet this racial memory lingered in me, had made the necessary electro-chemical connexions via the appropriate synapses in my soft brain, and the pictures in my head were as vividly and muddily real as Eastman Colour.

This present England was another kettle of fish entirely. Straight, linear, without U-turns. Obdurate and unyielding. Comprising black limos and *melyn cribos*. Helicopter gunships emitting symmetrical white shafts of several million candlepower. Huge screens and grotty stats and YOPs of shaved heads stamped with purple numbers. Starved rat terrorists and subversive cells. Toxic contamination we knew nothing of and wars we'd never heard about. Motorway flyovers ending in mid-air and signs pointing the way in but never the way out. Trouble was, this England existed only too literally. I couldn't escape it . . . and the new day that was dawning at last, by Govt decree, made it all the worse and too terribly real.

At the next stat, I decided, wherever that was, I would drop Brown, he was getting on my nerves. That performance with the radio! Who did he think he was trying to fool? Him and his friends would no more succeed in blowing up Dungeness B than assassinating the PM. I might come from the north but I wasn't born yesterday.

Amazingly I didn't feel tired any more. The *Temporal* must have done the trick, I congratulated myself. I also felt a surge of unfounded optimism, always the best sort.

This wasn't such a bad planet after all, I hummed to myself.

Something else I also now remembered: the boy or youth at Sandbach warning me about Watford Gap. Lucky we'd missed it during the longest night of my life. It was gone and forgotten, safely in the past behind us. As was the "deal" I had done with him, a favour for his friend Fully Olbin in exchange for the *Temporal*. Sucker!

Another such probable universe (the one I happened to be inhabiting) now hove into view in the broad light of day on the concrete horizon, and I grinned with relief at the sight.

The blue and white sign said: *Newport Pagnell Services*.

Not long after the sign flashed by we had to stop. Nothing wrong with the van, you understand, merely a build-up of traffic that stretched for what seemed miles ahead. I leaned out of the cab and called to a passenger in the adjacent car whose head lolled back on the padded headrest and whose rolling yellow eye regarded me balefully. He was in shirtsleeves, a hairy arm protruding out of the open window, and from my superior position I could see the straining girth of an expense-account belly overhanging his belt and straddling his knees.

"Excuse me, cock," I said, matching my tone to the outward show of my appearance and vehicle. "Why the hold-up?"

"Checkpoint."

"What checkpoint?"

"Anyone travelling south of Newport Pagnell has to pass through the checkpoint. Verify your papers are in order."

"What papers?"

"Resident Alien permit, National Insurance index, yellow card, Social Security number, National Health number, vehicle licence, road tax, insurance and MOT."

"Is that all?"

"Personal body check, belongings and baggage check, vehicle maintenance check, health clearance and AIDS screening."

79

"Is *that* all?"

"Rabies, firearms and explosive material, noxious or toxic substances, prohibited drugs, carcinogenic agents (asbestos, aerosols, etc), medical supplies and woodworkers' glue checks."

"That doesn't leave,—"

"Subversive or obscene printed material, *samizdat*, pirated audio and video cassette tapes, sexist literature, left wing or socialist-oriented brochures, pamphlets or tracts, statistical bulletins, private notebooks, personal letters, photographs and greetings cards of a dubious or doubtful nature."

"What else can they possibly,—"

"Political affiliations, trade union membership, associations, societies, clubs, pastimes, hobbies and recreational activities proscribed by Act of Parliament."

"Sure you haven't missed anything out?"

"Blood relations suffering or known to have suffered from diabetes, angina, liver trouble, leukemia, Parkinson's disease, Kaposi's sarcoma, piles, mental illness, insomnia . . ."

I wound the window up.

We tailgated at a snail's pace for about a mile, and with every metre nearer the checkpoint my trepidation increased logarithmically until I found myself in a sweating blue funk. Brown. He had to be got rid of. His mug and bio would be in their computer memory store. He would be detained and interrogated, and us, the Vail family, by association, with him. I could *glaswellt*, I supposed, and claim the reward, but how to explain we'd harboured a known subversive for nearly two hundred miles? Besides, he'd have his revenge by implicating us in his terrorist fantasies. He'd refer to us as "comrades" and eulogise our support and friendship, winking conspiratorially at the investigating officer and implying that Mira was a damn good *sqriw* (true, she was, biting, scratching, moaning fit to wake the dead) and that it was common practice in our "circle" to share the women like picnic food.

(Yes, and that was another reason why he deserved to be dumped without mercy,—his putative sexual congress with my wife. He had one hell of a nerve, after all I'd done for him, the swine.)

I told him to go, and to take his precious bloody bundle with him. I couldn't take the risk any longer. I had my family to consider. He replied that he could hide in the long drawer underneath the bunk, and I told him not to be such a bloody fool: the checkpoint guards would strip us down to the differential and filter the oil in the sump through muslin if need be. He was jeopardising our chances by remaining, didn't he see that? Where was his common decency, his sense of gratitude and brotherly concern? He didn't need me to give him lessons in *that*, he informed me brusquely. He hadn't noticed me overflowing with the milk of human kindness and compassion, not by a long chalk. Well, was he going to leave of his own accord or did I have to forcibly eject him? *Me* forcibly eject *him*? he scoffed. That'll be the day. I told him then and there that my patience was fast running out; moreover, I'd dealt with tougher cookies than him in my time, and if he wanted a physical confrontation he could have it, and welcome, in spades.

At this juncture in our heated exchange we were less than a mile from the checkpoint, inching forward amongst three solid lanes of nose-to-tail traffic. It was another hot day and the engine pulsating beneath me was an apt metaphor for my rage and frustration. Both of us, it seemed, were likely to explode at any moment.

Mira was saying something to Brown, too low for me to catch. Was she remonstrating with him, pleading with him, sympathising with him, imploring him to take her with him? Not the latter, I was certain: she was too attached to Bev.

As we crept past the half-kilometre marker I heard the side door slam and when I looked over my shoulder Brown had gone. Mira's remonstrances, pleadings, cajolings or whatever had ostensibly done the trick. We were rid of him at last! We could approach the checkpoint with confidence, secure in the knowledge that we had nothing to hide, were blameless of any crime against the state and could not be accused of subversive or terrorist affiliations. Involuntarily my shoulders sagged out of sheer relief. I said aloud,

81

"Thank God for that," but either Mira didn't hear or chose not to respond.

The guards were of the shiny black beetle variety, with tinted visors masking their eyes. Dutifully I followed the pointing black stun stick into the wire-mesh-enclosed bay and, obeying the sign, cut the engine. In the bay to our right a silver-grey Mercedes was ghosting through, not stopping, the occupants not even bothering to wind the windows down, and reclining in the back watching TV I recognised the familiar lithe form of Steve Davis, world champion snooker player and variety show guest star, clad in a dark-green polo-neck sweater, light-grey slacks and alligator-skin shoes decorated with little gold chains.

At his request I gave the guard all the papers we had. He thumbed through them and said, "Resident Alien permit, yellow card?"

"No. Sorry. You see, my daughter's ill and we're taking her,—"

He didn't even let me finish, but pointed with his stun stick to a slip road off to the left. "Move along."

"But isn't it possible,—"

"Move along, you're blocking traffic."

"Could I speak to someone in,—"

He gave me one look through the tinted visor and I started the engine and took the slip road to the left. The slip road curved back on itself and three hundred metres farther on we came to a roundabout signposted

A422 EAST →

← A422 WEST

M1 NORTH ↑

Most of the rejected traffic was taking the M1, but I was damned if I was going to give up so easily, and swung onto the A422 East and drove towards Bedford. Wrecks and abandoned vehicles lay on the grass verges at both sides of the road; other hopefuls, who had made it this far and no farther.

Mira remained silent, no doubt sick at heart that we'd failed to pass through. I hoped she wasn't going to blame it on me. I'd had a bellyful.

Periodically, to our right, glimpsed through trees and in-between buildings, I could see the wire topped with white ceramic insulators. It stayed in view for several miles until we reached a place called Bromham, a small village where the A422 meets the A428. At the crossroads there were signs pointing north to Northampton and Wellingborough and east to St Neots and Godmanchester. The signs to the south were plastered with large ACCESS RESTRICTED TO AUTHORISED VEHICLES notices, red letters on a white ground. Bedford itself was behind the wire inside this zone, and therefore off-limits.

I pulled over into a lay-by and switched off the engine. When I climbed stiffly and wearily into the back the reason for Mira's prolonged silence became apparent: she was casually sprawled out on the bunk opposite Bev, wearing blue lipstick which clashed badly with her bloodshot eyeballs staring up at me. There were no signs of struggle or sexual interference, though her fingers still clutched the flowered coverlet, and in places her nails had pierced through and were dug deep into the latex foam.

Around her throat, like a velvet choker, a thick black fabric belt (such as might have belonged to a heavy black overcoat) was tightly bunched and knotted behind her neck in a writhing thick black tangle in which some of her bleachily-streaked hair was trapped.

The three of us wandered the countryside in the vicinity of St Neots for a while, vainly seeking a way through, under or over the wire south, then towards the evening of the second day Mira began to smell and so I buried her. The logistical problems were becoming more and more acute. Petrol I could get, fairly easily, by the usual method, but food was dangerous. I didn't want to break into anyone's house for fear of getting shot, and the only other alternative was shop-lifting, which was nerve-racking business, I can tell you. I broke out in a sweat of panic fear every time I entered a shop, which was a dead giveaway. Something I learned to do was keep my mouth shut. In Waitrose I made the mistake of asking a woman where the dairy produce was and she reared back and regarded me flatly over her packed bosom and asked me where I came from. I indicated with my thumb a region somewhere over my right shoulder and said, "North."

"*The* North?"

I nodded without speaking.

"Thought so. I can see it in your face."

Instead of being circumspect and moving on I said rashly, "What can you see?"

"Workshy. Shiftless. Sneaky. Untrustworthy. Layabout."

"Oh?"

"You Held the Country to Ransom and Priced Britain Out of World Markets and now you're unemployed you're forever looking for State Handouts and Fiddling the Social Security and Sponging Off Society."

I now kept my mouth shut. Other people gathered as the woman went on:

"This Country doesn't Owe you a Living, you know. If you hadn't Wrecked Britain's Economic Performance with your Excessive Wage Demands and Restrictive Practices we might still have a Favourable Balance of Payments. As it is we're Bottom of the Uropean League Table, Begging for Crumbs at the Rich Man's Table."

Her face was round and smooth and high-coloured, polished to a sheen like a rosy apple. I had read Enid Blyton as a child and that's who she reminded me of, though I had no idea what Enid Blyton looked like. She wore a cardigan with pearl buttons fastened up to the neck and a fine woven houndstooth skirt with small pleats at either side.

Still I said nothing.

"What are you doing down here anyway? There's nothing for you here. We don't want your dirt and disease, your AIDS and Down's Syndrome. Get back up North where you belong."

"Yes, why *are* you here? What is it you want?" said a tall bleak man with spectacles and a lipless mouth whose jacket hung

84

emptily on him as on a coat-hanger. "Do as this lady says and return to those streets where one assumes you eat tripe and black puddings out of tin baths, don't wash your feet and wear flat caps in bed. Haven't you done enough harm?"

The lady in cardigan and houndstooth skirt said, "There's no reasoning with them. For generations they were kept in their place, docile, subservient, fawning, grateful for what they were allowed to have and we were generous enough to give them. Then they got ideas. I blame ITV. Can you imagine,—fitted carpets, central heating, freezers, video recorders and double glazing in a slum! The idea! Spoiled? I should indubitably say so!"

I had some vacuum-packed boiled ham inside my shirt and half a pound of foil-wrapped coffee in my underpants, so I thought it expedient not to refute these sentiments. I would have to shop-lift elsewhere for my dairy produce. I eased myself out of the crowd.

"See? Look at him, sloping off!" said another woman with snide gusto. She was younger than the first woman, and rather attractive, blonde hair swirled up onto the top of her dainty head and held in place by a diamanté comb. "Typical." She screwed up her face. "Bloody bolshie bastard!"

The tall bleak man poked a finger into me, just missing the boiled ham.

"You do realise what you've done, don't you? You and the rest of your lazy good-for-nothing pals? Sold This Country Down the River. That's what. Brought This Once-Proud Nation to its Knees. Well. I suppose you're happy now, aren't you? I suppose you're satisfied. I suppose you expect the rest of us to keep you in the style to which you've become accustomed, don't you?"

Enid Blyton kicked me on the shinbone. My gasp of pain triggered the latent fury residing a bare millimetre beneath the ordered, genteel exterior of these good people, causing someone at the back to throw a 500 ml carton of Cornish double cream which exploded and ejected its contents down the front of my shirt. Other esculent missiles followed in rapid, accurate succession, some of them hard such as jars of Chiver's thick cut marmalade, others soft and splattery: yoghurt, fruit, eggs, tomatoes, for example. I ran into the street stinking and afraid; they would have thrown warm turds had there been any to hand.

By sounding the long "a" and softening my speech to a suave murmur I succeeded in asking directions to the nearest hospital and received a helpful, non-hostile reply. The two-storey building was modern and new, set in its own grounds laid out with skill, expense and professional pride. There was even, as I recall, a small ornamental lake with weeping willows and lily pads.

It was dusk when I drove through the wrought-iron gates and parked between the yellow lines, covering over a stencilled hieroglyph which read: "AG/C2".

I wrapped Bev in a tartan blanket and carried her up the steps into the glazed reception hall. The doors slid open noiselessly at my approach and closed just as silently behind me. Neat wooden signs stuck out at right-angles along a restful green corridor, their black lettering sealed inside a coating of quick-wipe glare-free polyurethane: E.N.T., OCC. THERAPY, E.C.G., OPTH. SURG., SR. NRS. OFF., W.C. The lighting was of the diffused type so that it didn't hurt one's eyes. There was no one about.

I walked on the rubbery yielding floor, holding Bev firmly because it seemed that if I didn't she might float away. Her face had that translucent quality you might have seen in paintings of the madonna or in photographs of babies inside their mothers' wombs.

A heavy-busted nurse, all crackling starch and plastic pen-tops, passed directly across the corridor in front of me, in transit between wards, swivelled in mid-stride and came back to confirm her first subliminal impression.

"Might I inquire where you're taking that child?"

"Hello, nurse. This is my daughter, Bev. Could you find someone to attend to her? I think she's dying."

"Nonsense," the nurse said briskly, who according to her blue plastic name tab was Staff Nurse P. Bracegirdle. Without looking

86

at Bev, she said, "This isn't a casualty hospital. The nearest one is in Huntingdon. You can't miss it, it's directly off the A1."

"She isn't a casualty, she's dying," I said. "Please find a doctor. I'll wait here."

"Do you suppose that doctors are at your beck and call?" Her tone of voice was finely balanced between amused irony and a stern affront. Then, almost immediately, her precise eyebrows snapped together in an accusing frown. "You're not local. You don't sound local. Are you local?"

"Under the circumstances is it important? Please find a doctor for her. We can discuss my antecedents and geographical heritage later."

She didn't intend to budge, that much was plain. How long could we stand here, confronting one another? I stepped round her and continued on my way. Staff Nurse Bracegirdle came after me but drew the line at actually touching my stiff pungent shirt. She had caught a whiff of sour cream, eggs and yoghurt in my passing. We bandied more words, the upshot of which was that she backed away, both slender sanitised palms upraised, and said, "If you'll stay here and promise not to move I'll see if I can get someone."

Thus it was that I came to be ushered into the presence of Dr Tocktor, a small grey eminence sitting behind a plain bare desk in a tiny room with one window. It was dark outside, the curtains were undrawn, and in the hard black rectangle I could see myself mirrored holding a limp blanket in my arms.

Dr Tocktor didn't speak, merely pointed to a wooden chair. There were voices and footsteps in the corridor. The door opened and Staff Nurse Bracegirdle entered followed by three people in white coats, all of whom arranged themselves, standing, on either side of Dr Tocktor, which while bolstering his authority and prestige made him seem smaller, greyer, more shrunken than before. Almost insubstantial, in fact, so that in my fevered imagination I could see through him to the chair in which he sat.

"Doctor's waiting," said Staff Nurse Bracegirdle.

I began. "I would be most grateful, doctor, if you could spare the time to look at my daughter Bev. As you can see, she's very ill.

If she doesn't receive some attention soon she's going to die,—"

"Are you a doctor?" interrupted one of the others. I shook my head and this same person went on, "Dr Tocktor's had over twenty-five years' experience. A little bit more than you, I dare say."

I had to agree. "I'm sure the doctor is highly qualified,—"

"*Very* highly qualified," another of the people said. "No one has *ever* questioned Dr Tocktor's expertise and professional integrity in all the years he's been working here. He's noted for it."

"I'm glad to hear it."

"And so you should be."

"I am,—"

"Twenty-five *years*," said Staff Nurse Bracegirdle vehemently. "Have you any idea of the sacrifices and dedication and heartaches that has entailed? The exams he had to pass, the years of penny-pinching, the bone-weary hours late at night when he was dead on his feet and would have loved a long hot soak and a good night's sleep but had to carry on regardless till the early hours of the morning? You can't conceive."

"No, I can't," I admitted. "I'm sure the doctor is everything you say he is—very highly qualified, with long experience, expert and dedicated and so on."

There were one or two satisfied nods. They had made their point.

Dr Tocktor hadn't spoken a word or moved a muscle during this. He was gazing in my general direction but not quite at me, at a spot on the wall about nine or ten inches to my left. Had he taken any of this in? I wondered. Was he with us in spirit if not in the flesh?

"What's the matter with daughter?" asked one of the standing people.

"I don't know, I'm not a doctor," I said. "But I think,—that is, I believe, I'm of the opinion,—that she's dying."

"And what has led you to this 'opinion'?" Staff Nurse Bracegirdle asked, a snide smile shimmering at the corners of her immaculate lips. I thought I saw her nudge one of the others playfully.

"You only have to look at her. She has sores on her face, neck and chest. She's down to less than three stone. She's been in a coma for the past four days. She has a temperature, her breathing is very shallow and her pulse is weak."

"So you think she might be ill."

"Yes. I'm not an expert,—"

"We've established that," said one. "Doctor is the expert. It's up to him to decide whether daughter's ill or not. In this hospital we do things by the book."

A lengthy silence ensued. I could hear the ticking of Dr Tocktor's watch on his thin grey wrist. Were they waiting for me? I'd explained the symptoms, there was nothing more to say. I racked my brains. Should I tell them I'd given her *Temporal*? No, they'd frown on that, on a lay person administering unauthorised drugs without proper medical supervision. I waited some more. It seemed that several minutes elapsed, though it was probably only three or four.

Footsteps went by outside, metallic and feminine, and I heard a voice say, "Oh, Miss Marsh, a word . . ."

"How long has daughter been like this?" one or other wanted to know. I broke out of the light trance I'd fallen into and said, "Several weeks at least. I should say two months, give or take a week or two."

Staff Nurse Bracegirdle worked her tongue behind her lower lip and wormed it to the side of her mouth so that her cheek bulged with sardonic mischief. "Rather vague, aren't we?" she said with a raised eyebrow. "My goodness. 'Give or take a week or two.' That could mean almost anything."

"Well," I said, "some considerable time anyway. The symptoms came on slowly."

"That's even vaguer," another scoffed. "'Some considerable time' and 'slow symptoms',—whatever they are,—aren't a recognised part of medical parlance. You might just as well have said, 'I haven't a clue' or 'I can't remember' for all the help that is. Doctors should know better."

"I'm not a doctor," I said.

"We've established that," Staff Nurse Bracegirdle said with a touch of asperity bordering on irritation. "What we're saying is not doctors *ought* to know better but doctors *should* know better, and they do. You're not denying that, I hope?" Again the condescendingly amused crinkle at the corner of her mouth.

The grey incorporeal shadow that was Dr Tocktor turned its head to one side and the four staff in attendance leaned forward in collective reverence. The doctor's thin lips didn't move, or if they did I didn't see them; yet Staff Nurse Bracegirdle straightened up and requested that I move my chair farther back.

"Back where?"

"Away from the desk."

"How far away?"

"Twenty-five centimetres or ten inches."

I complied by edging the chair back the required distance with the backs of my knees and sat down again. Dr Tocktor, I now noticed, was looking directly at me,—still not into my eyes, but at the centre of my forehead. Were we getting somewhere at last?

"If you would consider admitting my daughter for observation," I ventured, "I'm positive you'll discover that she really is in a very serious condition."

The four exchanged surprised if rather tolerant looks.

One or other said, "Well, that's something of an advance, I suppose. At least now he's *positive*. Before it was merely a 'belief', an 'opinion'. Well, well. What is it they say,—a little knowledge is a dangerous thing?"

"Learning."

"Are you a doctor?" Staff Nurse Bracegirdle flashed.

"No," I said. "Sorry."

"Who is the doctor?"

"Him."

"*Him!*"

"Dr Tocktor."

"It would be well for you to remember that. You haven't been secretly trying to edge your chair nearer the desk, have you?"

I shook my head.

"We're watching. We can tell. None of us are fools here. We're all very highly qualified and very experienced. Just remember that."

Dr Tocktor looked at his watch, the cue for Staff Nurse Bracegirdle to say briskly: "Come. You've taken up enough of doctor's valuable time. I'm sure daughter isn't as bad as you make out. Give her a Panadol or one of those similar kinds of small round white tablets and let her sleep it off. Plenty of fluids. Keep her bowels open. In the morning all your fears will be foolish daydreams. Take doctor's word for it."

Someone tapped on the door and a hand thrust a paper in which Staff Nurse Bracegirdle snatched and read. "Are you the owner of a green Bedford van, registration FTJ 109V that was parked in the space reserved for AG/C2?"

I shook my head. "No. *Is* parked in that space. I parked it there myself."

"Not any longer. AG/C2 arrived and had the police remove it. It's been impounded. Come along," she bustled, "doctor has other patients to see besides daughter. I think you've had more than your fair share, don't you?"

She escorted me to the entrance and what she said was true: a metallic blue Volvo Estate with tinted sunroof and Disneyland stickers in the back window was occupying the space where the van had been. The glass doors slid soundlessly shut behind me as I walked down the steps carrying the tartan blanket in my arms. And would you believe it,—after all these days of fine sunny weather it was starting to spit.

Bends and hills were pure torture. At every turn in the road I had to hold my breath as a tidal wave rippled and sloshed the length of the tank and went over my head. Bad enough to be drowned, you might suppose, but it was *icy* cold into the bargain and I had lost all feeling in my feet, and my hands gripping the aluminium struts were frozen into claws.

When the tanker went downhill and its liquid load submerged me for lengthy periods of time I just had to hang there in the freezing darkness, lungs aching, and pray that the hill was of short duration. Going uphill was easier, because then the load shifted to the rear and left my head clear above the white frothing surface. But the cold was the worst, I can tell you.

Coming out of the woods I had seen the United Dairies' tankers being filled under floodlights at the depot. Thirty or more were lined up behind a chain-link fence, their round stainless steel lids open at an angle like tank hatches in war films, and it had been child's play to scale the fence, climb the short ladder to the fretted catwalk of the nearest tanker and drop down into the empty blackness inside. At this point I was warm, perspiring from my exertions; but that soon changed when they began to pump it in, refrigerated to bollock-shrinking level.

When it reached my chest I got worried, and when it lapped my chin I panicked.

By then I was floating with my head bumping the roof. If they filled it snug to the brim that would be that, I remember thinking, the end of the line for the Vail family: one strangled and buried just off the A422, another tenderly smothered in a tartan blanket and placed under stones reverently piled in a wood somewhere (I had no implement with which to dig a hole), the third drowned in milk.

My bequest to the nation would be several thousand noses wrinkling over their breakfast cornflakes and a stack of complaints to the Customer Liaison Officer of United Dairies.

The tanker passed through the wire just north of Sandy on the A1 in the very early hours of a drizzly August morning. My choice of transport, as it turned out, had been most opportune: commercial vehicles entering the South were subjected to an X-ray scan to detect arms shipments and stowaways, but milk was exempt from this regulation due to reasons of possible spoilage.

In this manner I arrived in London, safe, in one piece, but suffering from frostbite.

3RD SECTION   LONDON (II)

[1]

Vail is washing the dishes, dusting the furniture and Hoovering the floor when Pete Rarity rings him up to tell him that Bryce Ransom is impressed with him and would like to arrange an interview. Pete Rarity sounds as pleased as if he were the one going for the interview, absolutely chuffed about it. The thing that discomfits Vail is that although he has made it perfectly plain that he doesn't like Pete Rarity, hates him, positively detests him, this doesn't deter Pete Rarity one little bit. Pete Rarity can't fail to know that Vail can't stand the sight of him, yet he hangs around, rings up for drinks and so on, all the while acting as if he and Vail were the best of chums, and Vail is at a loss to know what to do about it.

He will come upon Vail in a supermarket, say, and thrust his face into Vail's with heroic cheerfulness and a breezy, "Hello, John, how are you! Long time no see. How are you doing? How are things going? Are you well? What's happening?"

As very little of any consequence is happening in Vail's life, his response is invariably to shrug and mumble a few phrases and move on to the tinned fruit, searching for Bartlett pears in syrup, a delicacy Angie is unable to live without apparently.

"Why does he want to see me?" Vail asks, silencing the Hoover with his toe. "We hardly exchanged three words and I didn't understand any of them."

"Who cares why, it's a Golden Opportunity," Pete Rarity tells him breathlessly. "He must have seen something in you."

The prospect of an Opportunity, Golden or otherwise, attracts Vail. And what has he to lose? Only his Hoover, his apron, and his dishpan hands.

"You mentioned an interview."

93

"That's right."

"When? Where?"

"Thames. Thursday. Eleven."

"Will you be there?"

"Me? *Me?*" Pete Rarity laughs raucously. "Bry wouldn't invite me. He thinks I'm a pillock."

"Are you?"

"Bry seems to think so. Besides, I'm too ugly to appear on television. Frighten the horses."

"What do you mean, 'on television'? He doesn't want me to appear on television, does he?"

"Why not, John? You're presentable. You've got what it takes. Bry's an ace spotter, I'll say that for him. He saw something in you and he wants to exploit it."

"I'm not exploitable."

"Let Bry be the judge of that. Place yourself in his capable hands. You won't regret it!"

Angie is all for it, says, "You can get your yellow card, ever think of that? Television companies can fix *anything* short of assassinations. They make or break people just like that." She snaps her fingers. "Take your apron off and let's have sex. I've been panting for it all day while poring over proofs. We'll do it on the carpet."

"I've just Hoovered," Vail objects.

"All right, in bed. Get the Bartlett pears. Afterwards we can read John Folwes together and fall asleep in each other's arms."

Just as sex equates Bartlett pears in Angie's philosophy, sleep equates John Folwes in Vail's.

Reports on the 5.45 news include radiation leakage at Dungeness B, which turns out to be a scare story put about by irresponsible elements, the PM in Geneva to receive the World Peace and Social Harmony Prize, a man with no arms and legs who started his own computer software company, the world famous swimmer and sportswoman Sharon Davis signing an advertising endorsement contract worth half-a-million dollars, and questions raised in Parliament about the deteriorating quality of Britain's milk. "As if a tramp had been swimming in it with his socks on," complained one distraught MP, several of whose Surrey constituents had written to him to say that it had made them quite ill.

This is followed by a quiz show, *Feet 'n' Porridge*, in which contestants have to identify the naked feet of various entertainers and showbiz celebrities in exchange for lavish prizes; however if they get it wrong they have to wade up to their knees through a trough of cold porridge while singing a song or reciting a poem. Vail gets two right, and had he been a contestant would have won a fortnight's holiday for two in Santiago.

"Nothing on the news about your wife and kid," Angie remarks. "They can't have decomposed yet, so they mustn't have been found." She strokes his bare thigh in the tiny cluttered bedroom. They aren't, strictly speaking, "in bed", because there is no bed, just a mattress on the dusty floorboards underneath a shadeless bulb pumping out all of forty watts of electrical energy.

"It happened on the other side of the wire," Vail reminds her. "Probably censored."

"This is a democracy don't forget," Angie says, licking the inside of his leg with a pointed tongue, "with a free press. No murder goes unreported, especially a grisly one involving the working classes."

"What about the deliberate dumping of toxic chemicals and radioactive waste in densely-populated areas? Why don't they report that?"

"Rumour and hearsay. It's more than a journalist's job's worth to print stuff not properly authenticated and verified by independent sources. In addition you have to have balance. Without balance all is chaos," she says, nuzzling his scrotum. "Remember what Lord Reith said."

"What?"

"I forget now, but it was crucially important. It set the standard for all that was to follow."

95

"All what that was to follow?" asks Vail, genuinely puzzled.

"Can't talk," Angie mumbles indistinctly. "Mouth full." And so it is, Vail discovers, easing back with a silent gasp against the pillows.

[2]

The heat in the capital seems to have dissipated. People are still making money hand over fist however. Computer, video and sex shops doing a roaring trade, etc. The cooler weather doesn't appear to affect them one way or the other. Consumption and titillation thrive in all temperatures.

At Thames (yet more glazed reception areas, this time with jungle foliage) Vail sinks deep into a sofa while he waits to be called. He muses on the irony of being taken up by Bryce Ransom when he himself entertained no such desire or intention. Others were clamouring to be let in, lying, cheating, stealing and fornicating for the whiff of a chance to achieve admittance to the white hot centre of the universe, and were left standing on the pavement outside while he, a down-and-out, a no-hoper, a fringer, had been granted the Golden Opportunity.

He looks up to see Lyndsey de Paul, hair cascading her shoulders, walk through with a tall bearded man wearing a gold earring. They are in animated conversation. The bearded man says something amusing and the talented singer-songwriter laughs with her pretty red mouth and beautiful teeth.

My God thinks Vail, *I could meet somebody famous here. I could actually converse with them, crack a joke, and they might even laugh. Their worlds and mine intersecting—incredible thought! I could watch them eating in the canteen and observe them on the way to the lavatory. Still,* he reflects, *television stars and top entertainers have to defecate like the rest of us. Unreasonable to expect otherwise.*

Vail is directed to Room 606 where Bryce Ransom, temples throbbing, spectacles glinting, pounces on him and drags him by the arm to a leather couch which sucks him in with much creaking and escaping of stale air.

"Impossible trying twat in for all of us combined. Asked me *twice* to cut but interference scheduling cock-ups as per semblance of priorities. I wouldn't could but do he? Could he slag off Studio 9 in place? Could he mustn't. Anyway, last time ducks out isn't for want of piling agony, even through bread in his mouth wouldn't cunt if it was or didn't. Tea or coffee?"

"Coffee without milk," Vail says thankfully, both for the offer and for having understood three words from this torrent of gibberish.

Already he is getting a headache in dreadful anticipation of more of the same. He can't last out, he knows this. Another half-hour of Bryce Ransom and Vail will leap through the double glazing to the paved forecourt six floors below. Either that or throttle him with the stringy tie that the entertainment producer wears loosely knotted around his perpendicular veined neck.

Bryce Ransom gulps scalding coffee. His thin mat of forward-brushed hair reminds Vail of a sparse covering of grass on top of a limestone cliff. The face trapped inside the wire spectacle frames is twitchy with spasms of uncontrollable brain impulses. Probably Bryce Ransom doesn't himself understand half of what he's saying; probably it doesn't matter, and even if it does, who cares?

Further torrents ensue, during which Vail detects continual references to one Virgie Hance; though who this Virgie Hance is and what he has to do with Vail's visit, Vail can't decipher. By the sound of him he's American, and the speculation enters Vail's mind that he's about to be flown out to Hollywood, all expenses paid, to undergo plastic surgery on his teeth. Perhaps Bryce Ransom is talent-spotting for this Virgie Hance person, and perhaps he isn't, it's anybody's guess.

This state of affairs can't go on for much longer because Vail really does have a headache now, a real beauty, and is rapidly nearing the leaping-through-double-glazing or throttling-with-stringy-tie point of the interview, and this after barely ten minutes.

"Impetus counts could nullify if not precautions, especially at the time dreaming fat fuck, isn't?" Bryce Ransom asks rhetorically, making Vail grind his teeth in impotent rage. This was as bad as,—worse than,—discussing the erotic symbolism of John Folwes with Angie. How could Thames employ such a person? Surely all television producers didn't speak in this fashion?

The lean and rangy producer suddenly reaches out at full stretch and presses a tab on the intercom, shirt riding up his back to reveal a slice of pale freckled flesh. There is a brief staccato exchange and he coils back to sit beside Vail on the creaking leather sofa, a smile straining his skinny rawboned face.

He nods alertly at Vail. "Okay true?"

"Yes. Sure. Why not?" What has he let himself in for now? Vail wonders dismally. He half-expects the door to burst open and a red-haired woman come striding in with a cigarette dangling from the corner of her mouth like a Liverpool docker.

This is what does, in fact, happen.

Before he can rise, out of politeness, the woman is pumping his hand and observing him shrewdly through eyes screwed up against the shroud of cigarette smoke. She is young, thirtyish or thereabouts, quite slim, with gaps separating her teeth. She is attractive when she doesn't speak and terrifyingly frightful when she does. Her voice and manner obliterate all feminineness, yet her physical body is desirable. Vail desires and is revulsed all at once.

"Have a good trip? Bry's told me all about you. Where are you staying? Sorry I couldn't meet you. Where do you want to eat? I know a little place. Pity you can't join us, Bry. You're not going to quibble over money, I hope. Hell of a tight schedule. You're not under contract to anyone? Bastard to park round here. No doubt Bry's told you already. We'd better chat. Where's your coat? We can walk from here. Service is lousy but the wine's superb. How tall are you? Listen, we'd best be going. Will you be around later, Bry? Week 14, don't forget. See you later. Are you coming? We can talk on the hoof."

They are along the corridor, down in the lift, across the

98

reception hall and out into the street walking fast before Vail has time to put lard on the cat's boil.

The wine bar is plush with polished brass rails and deep beige carpets, even in the gent's toilet. Lithe-hipped waiters steal about. Vail orders avacado salad, which arrives in sufficient quantity to feed a family of four. The red-haired woman has a sliver of fish accompanied by a splodge of pink speckled sauce. Bottles of wine and Perrier appear and disappear with astonishing rapidity. Vail's head swims. He has to summon up all his powers of concentration to take in what the red-haired woman is saying, the gist of which, it transpires, has something to do with the fact that she is seeking someone to "front" a television programme whose subject, or theme, is aggressive self-reliance. The title of the programme is *Bootstraps*, which puts Vail in a quandary, because he can't make the connexion between aggressive self-reliance and trapping boots. But then all television people (the two of his acquaintance) seem to talk in a code that excludes the greater part of humanity.

"You want me at the front of this programme," Vail says, trying not to slur his speech.

"No, I want you to front it."

"I see." (He doesn't.)

"Are those your own teeth? That shirt and those pants will do fine. Who's your agent? Have some more Perrier. Do you like this place? I was in LA recently, you know. When can you start? Camera test and production meeting next Thursday suit? This is delicious, how's the salad?"

She spears a piece of fish and blows smoke from the corner of her mouth, takes a gulp of wine and puts the fish in her mouth and chews it while taking a quick drag with a sudden sharp intake of breath, dabbing her chin with a napkin through the cigarette smoke.

"Will I get paid for this?" Vail asks, bleary-eyed.

"Minimum contract with stipulations and options. Three days' growth of beard at least. The primitive look. More wine, waiter. Don't lose the accent. Don't endorse anything, not yet. Spoil the image. Who's your accountant?"

She waves to someone at another table and leans closer.

"Current affairs at Central. Swine. Dessert or coffee? Leave the hair alone. Six weeks possibly extended to thirteen. Any commitments? I'll have a brandy, I think. What are you doing this evening?"

"I don't have a yellow card."

"Immaterial."

"Will you investigate my past?"

"Will if you want us to." The red-haired woman looks at the man's watch on her wrist. "Coffee? Brandy? Milk?"

Vail says uncertainly, "I'm not sure about this, Miss . . ."

"Mzzz."

"I'm not sure about this, Miss Mzzz." Vail feels sick.

"Then don't have anything if you don't want. Coffee, brandy and milk aren't everyone's cup of tea. Two thirty-seven."

"About the job."

"What about it? Have a mint."

"Will I be recognised in the street?"

"Who by? Waiter!"

"It could prove embarrassing."

"People aren't that easily embarrassed nowadays." She lights a cigarette and puts it in the corner of her mouth, which means she now has a cigarette in each corner. She removes the shorter of the two and stubs it out in the overladen ashtray, sending up a cloud of ash, and bats it aside.

"Shacked up with anyone?"

"Are you sure I'm the man you want?"

"Oh yes. Definitely. Will you take American Express?"

"Pardon?"

But she is speaking to the waiter hovering at Vail's shoulder, who scoops up the plastic card on a silver tray and dematerialises.

Vail believes it is time for some plain speaking. He launches in. "Look, Miss Mzzz, I don't want to seem ungrateful,—"

"Miss Mzzz?" laughs the red-haired woman, revealing all the gaps between her teeth. "I'm Mzzz Hance."

"Hance?"

"Virgie Hance. Short for Virginia."

100

"*You're* Virgie Hance?"

"Absolutely. Always have been." She grasps his wrist in a grip of steel. "What about tonight? Are we on?"

"You mean . . ."

"My friend's in Chicago on business. Just you and me." Her eyes bore into him. Her choppers gleam. He is gazing into the mouth of Hell. "Lord Napier Place, Upper Mall. Service entrance, nine o'clock. Stretched out on the rug, telly off, stereo on. And take your time, I'm a slow comer."

"I've just lost my wife."

"She'll turn up again. Nine o'clock. Bring an erection."

[3]

A person or persons unknown had been trying to get in touch with Vail on the telephone. He, she or they wouldn't leave their name(s), and this Vail found unsettling. Was it a lone psychotic or an organised group? There were millions of cranks in the world,—stood to reason he would get his fair share. Still, he didn't like it. His past was too near for him to breathe easy.

Also, events had moved fast. It seemed to Vail that he had been taken in hand by people and forces beyond his control. Not that he objected to this: he was of a mind to be swept along willy-nilly, the pawn of obsessional careerists, sexually ambitious women, and the whimsical ebb and flow of arbitrary circumstances. In his numbed state it was a relief to, as it were, let go. Sooner or later an Opportunity would present itself, of this he was confident.

—No, he didn't believe in justice, but he believed in good and evil, and just as in nature every action has an opposite and equal reaction, the callous and the sordid and the meretricious were ultimately balanced and rectified by other, positive forces, completing the algebraic equation, wiping the slate clean. This was so, had to be so, otherwise the universe would not function, would collapse under the weight of its own inertia, spiralling downwards into entropy and annihilation.

101

[*It doesn't occur to Vail that this may be the truth of the matter: that the exquisite symmetry of the atoms and the majesty of celestial engineering are a shameless hoax, a blatant deceit, and that we are all doomed to the pit. An electromagnetic god is no respecter of moral stances. Who is to say, in a purposeless universe, that we shall not all end up squashed flat like gnats? Ask a squashed gnat what it thinks of moral stances and you will get a dusty answer.*]

[4]
ANOTHER ATTEMPT
ON PM'S LIFE!

screams the hoarding. Vail orders the Merc to pull over. The newsboy, a man in his fifties with a knobbly face and bad teeth, stares at Vail transmogrified and touches the peak of his cap. Vail parts with a pound coin and waves away the change elegantly. The Merc re-enters the heavy flow of traffic.

"I tink he wreck'nised you, bawz," says the big black chauffeur with a split melon grin. He is six-feet-four, wears a grey uniform with tightly-buttoned collar, breeches and polished knee boots with swinging gold tassels.

Vail has been advised that he needs such a person for protection. But protection from what, from whom?

"You need to be handled," Virgie Hance has told Vail fiercely. "And who better to handle you than the Ed Flesh Personality Promotions Agency? He's a smart cookie. None smarter."

Ed Flesh is small and slim and softly spoken, Vail discovers. He is the brother of a famous comedian and was once a television director, which didn't satisfy his mad lust for power, wealth and prestige, in that order. He wears smoothly expensive suits and never raises his voice above an artificially cultured murmur. Hence the things he has to say are doubly impressive and shocking.

102

"We can push your gross up to one hundred grand minimum and launder it through an endowment trust so you don't have to pay tax. Endorsements in the first annum could realise thirty to forty K; book, recording and video advances about the same. Journalism doesn't pay much but it's good profile-building. We take a twenty-five per cent cut off the top, thirty per cent of overseas and US earnings. We might try for charitable status, which means you're exempt from tax and VAT and can invite contributions from the public. You'll need image-enhancement and protection and a press cuttings service. We can provide them for an additional five per cent of gross. Libel suits, litigation and writs you settle out of your own pocket. If you need to dry out, kick the habit, go into an AIDS clinic or require under-age sex, we can handle it. Glad to have you aboard. Sign here."

"What about my past?"

"I'll have our writers work one up for you. Fill in the questionnaire before you leave."

It is a rare day when Ed Flesh smiles and today is no exception. He smokes large cigars which make his hands and head look small. He sits behind a large empty desk which reinforces this impression. The illusion is that of a man seen through the wrong end of a telescope; Vail feels he ought to yell and scream at the top of his lungs in order to be heard by this diminutive figure sitting marooned on the far side of an acre of glass-topped walnut veneer. Yet Ed Flesh's low, modulated, reasonable voice reaches Vail easily, without undue strain.

"The first step is a complete biophysical profile for the press launch. Shots of you sleeping in a cardboard box under a railway viaduct, eating out of dustbins, on your knees licking grease from discarded chip-wrappings in Trafalgar Square late at night, that sort of thing. Perhaps interfering with a child in a public place, although we'll have to give that some thought. We don't want to tarnish any potential sex image. Kicking an old lady along the gutter would be safer. Nothing homosexual, I don't think. No, too alienating. Then we move onto the gradual process of rehabilitation. You sell French ticklers to Japanese tourists in

103

Leicester Square. Each item carries a one hundred and forty per cent mark-up and you plough back the profits and open your first shop in Islington. You buy up a shipment of Taiwanese video porn dirt cheap and rent a booth in Charing Cross Road and clear your entire stock in under two weeks, which gives you the working capital to rent larger premises in Greek Street. You now have two shops and a booth and employ five people, and three months later it's five shops and three booths employing twenty-seven people, plus your own warehousing facility. You begin to diversify. You move into sexual prosthetics for disabled Falklands servicemen. For this you need your own injection-moulding and extrusion plant, and very soon you find yourself supplying inductance capacitance cores to Sinclair for flat-screen TV production and plastic formes for anti-personnel landmines to the MoD. Within a year, we'll make that eighteen months, you're a self-made millionaire with houses, cars, yachts, Learjet, so on and so forth. You still jog and you're into aerobics. Whims and charming idiosyncracies are standing in the crowd at a football match when you can afford an executive box, hell, the whole damn stand, and taking your kids by Rolls to Battersea Fun Fair on Easter Sunday. The public loves that common detail. It leads them to believe you're still human and have ordinary feelings.''

"I don't have any children," Vail feels like yelling at the small man, but constrains himself to speaking normally.

Ed Flesh reaches below the desk with a miniature manicured hand and brings up a leather ring binder containing colour photographs of children sealed inside clear plastic. "Pick one of each, aged twelve and seven. Of you could have adopted a half-caste Indonesian kid whose parents got wiped out in a drought. That gives you heart with a capital h."

"What about a wife?"

"Would you like one?"

"Well, I thought with two kids . . ."

"Smart thinking. However,—a wife knocks the PSA on the head, which is a prime factor. Consider that?"

No, Vail hasn't considered that, for the simple reason that he doesn't know what Ed Flesh is talking about. "PSA?" he inquires diffidently.

"Puberulent Sexual Angle. Girls of the pre- and post-pubertal period, or P-4, don't relate to men with wives. We'll never get them to cough up £5 a year fan club membership if you're happily married. And presupposing a bottom line of 30,000 units, that could mean one hundred and fifty grand down the chute over a guesstimated three years."

"Do I need a fan club?"

"Do you need hot raunchy sex with a big-titted black chick every other day? Of course you need a fan club. It's the base for your merchandising programme. Vail pics, Vail discs, Vail videos, Vail ashtrays, Vail egg cups, Vail tablelamps, Vail pizzas, Vail lawnmowers,—"

"I can't help feeling this is getting a bit out of hand, Mr Flesh."

"Call me Flesh."

"Flesh."

"What's getting a bit out of hand?"

"Will pre- and post-pubertal girls really go for this stuff?"

"What stuff?"

"Egg cups and lawnmowers."

"I was speaking metaphorically. This has got to go through our market research department before we select key target groups. The P-4 rating could be the wrong one for you, we don't know yet. We have to run your BPP through the Apple and see what it comes up with."

"BPP?"

"Biophysical Profile Potential. Did you know I was the brother of a famous comedian who has since died?"

"I think Mzzz Hance may have mentioned it. What did he die of?"

"What do all famous comedians die of? Drugs and alcohol necessitated by unsatisfactory personal relationships and a broken marriage."

A hidden telephone rings and Ed Flesh picks up the receiver

from a recess on the side of the desk. He listens and then speaks. "Input incurs if you haven't otherwise, but never mind why Selina mustn't. Drop it through twat and cancel Week 14, preferably instant access maybe shouldn't she could. Simple deviant."

"Bryce Ransom?" Vail says when Ed Flesh has concluded the conversation.

"He wants to book Selina for *Feet 'n' Porridge* but her toes are already under contract to Coty."

"Is there any of her that's free?" Vail asks out of curiosity.

"That's the problem. We've sold most of the bits of her and there isn't much left. The poor kid's in twenty different places at once as it is. He can have her knees but that would mean changing the format, which Bry is loath to do."

"What about her ears?" Vail suggests helpfully.

"Sony."

"Elbows?"

"Martini."

"Back of her neck?"

"Bergasol."

"Cunt?"

"C.U.N.T."

"Pardon?"

"Conservative United National Trust."

"Liver?"

"Pedigree Chum."

"Spleen?"

"National Listeners' and Viewers' Association."

"Not much left," Vail sympathises.

"Not a fat lot," Ed Flesh agrees philosophically. "Her nipples are worth their weight in Uranium 235. What about those phone calls you've been getting?"

"Phone calls?"

"People ringing you up and refusing to leave their name or names."

"How do you know about them?"

"Naturally your phone is tapped. Your problems are our

106

problems, your life is our life, your phone calls are our phone calls. Leave us to deal with it."

"How?"

"Trust Forte. We can put our security and surveillance people onto it."

"Who's that?"

"Wayde Dake Ass. Inc. They'll trace the calls to source and deal unceremoniously with the perpetrators. You have to protect your image, Jack, now that you're in the public eye. Just say the word."

Vail nods, though none too happily. He doesn't like receiving phone calls from a person or persons unknown, but he likes even less the prospect of discovering who he, she or they might turn out to be.

From the inset speakers either side of Vail's head issue the muted tones of Jimmy Young interviewing a cabinet minister. The atmosphere is jocund and cosily intimate and JY concludes the interview with a cheery "Don't leave it too long next time, Keith. Cheers. 'Bye."

Then the sound of The Pox singing their latest chartbuster, *One For All and All For Freedom* infiltrates the padded interior, a protest ditty whose lyrics are concerned with the fate of dissidents in distant lands.

> "Saw it in the paper yesterday
> Somebody killed half a world away
> Shot in the back in broad daylight
> Killed for what he believed to be right.
>
> Chile, Argentina, El Salvador
> The Philippines, Uganda, East Timor
> The names mean nothing to you and me
> We're blind to the reason oh can't you see."

Vail turns it off and reads about the latest attempt on the PM's life.

"Who dat dey say respons'bull, bawz?"

"The INLA, the Libyans, the CNI, the Red Brigade, Black September,—"

"All of dem?" says the chauffeur, rolling his eyes.

"One or the other, they're not sure which."

"Dey sure am bad people, dem teachers."

"Oh?"

"Wouldn't cha tink dey'd act more respons'bull, dem folks on de Inner London Ed'cashun Aut-ority, what wid all der ed'cashun?" He shakes his vast head sadly. "What in de world is de world coming to, lawd a' mercy me, I don' know."

"They're up in arms," Vail tries to explain, "about the cutbacks."

"De gov'ment cutting back on de Red Brigade?" the chauffeur says in tones of amazement, steering carefully round a bomb crater outlined with flapping orange flags. "Why dey do dat?"

"No, the INLA."

"*Dey* cutting back on de Red Brigade?" More amazement.

"No, it's the INLA who are up in arms about the cutbacks; that's why they tried to shoot the PM."

"Dat's a cryin' shame, bawz. De PM ain't to blame." Something else seems to be bothering the chauffeur. "But why de business folks involve demselves in dis ruckus?" he wants to know. "Dey bein' cut back too?"

"What business folks?"

"Dose Confed'rashun business people."

"The CNI, you mean?" The chauffeur nods. "That is a puzzle," Vail admits, and frowns. "Unless they're not getting the subsidies they're entitled to. It's a very complicated situation."

"You can say dat 'gain, bawz. I'se utterly baffled, buggered and bewildered by all dese politacul goin's on."

So is Vail, though he does his best, from his meagre store of knowledge, to elucidate:

"As I understand it, there are various groups, or factions, or cells, attempting to overthrow the *status quo*. They all have the same object in mind, though for different purposes. None of them, apparently, gets on with any of the others. Why I don't know, so don't ask me. Some of them are a bit upset because Urop was devastated by a nuclear blast and the Govt refuses to admit it . . ."

"Devastated?" the chauffeur interrupts, glancing at Vail in the mirror. "Is dat de same as destroyed? Urop bin destroyed? Since when? I ain't read 'bout dat."

"No, you won't have because the Govt won't admit it. That's why the factions are a bit upset."

"No damn wonder."

"You could say dat. That."

"When dis happen?"

"Nobody seems to know. Perhaps it never did happen,—hasn't happened yet, I mean. Some factions insist that it did, others disagree."

"Don't nobody know for sure? Either it did or it didn't, can't be no two ways 'bout it."

"Then there's the Libyans."

"How dey come into dis?"

Vail thinks hard, trying to remember what he has been told. "I seem to recall they were working hand-in-glove with the INLA."

"What dem Libbys and de Inner London Ed'cashun Aut-ority got in common, for de lawd's sake? Dey's poles apart, seems to I. Dis is very confusin', bawz."

Vail has to agree. And how did toxic waste and radioactivity fit into the picture? Were the Red Brigade and Black September trying to spread the contamination or contain it? Could they be described as urban guerrillas, freedom fighters, subversive terrorists or what? And who was funding them,—the Confederation of British Industry? And supposing they did succeed in overthrowing the *status quo*, what then? Would the British Isles be devastated as allegedly Urop had been? His head was starting to throb and he hoped the chauffeur wouldn't ask any more questions; how had they started this conversation in the first place?

The city unfolds around them like a sour dream. A yellowish miasma (toxic pollution? acid rain? radiation cloud?) hides the sun.

Yet the people in the streets are fat and sleek and prosperous and the tourists are buying up Oxford Street as though there were no tomorrow. Perhaps they know something?

The Merc is diverted round the sterile area of Knightsbridge by a police roadblock. Now that Harrods has an average of ten bomb alerts and three actual blasts a week it is no longer permissable to approach within one hundred yards of the proud and battered building except on foot, and then only after a rigorous body search. Vail had paid a visit two or three days ago. It was a sight and a symbol that brought a mist of patriotic fervour to the eyes of any true Brit.

Huge banners draped across the cracked and shattered face of the building proclaimed: GRAND RE-RE-RE-OPENING (the third, in fact, this week) and BUSINESS AS USUAL and WE NEVER HAVE AND NEVER WILL CLOSE. A fortune was being spent on the continuous rebuilding and refurbishing programme. Hours after the latest current blast the builders and glaziers and decorators moved in to repair the damage. A special high-powered Govt fund had been set up,—chaired by a cabinet minister,—which promised to match penny for penny what was raised by public donations. Millions poured in every week. Those damn subversive scum would never make the country's finest and most famous emporium, with its decades of heritage and tradition of doughty British trading, knuckle under to cowardly terrorist blackmail. Just who did these spineless greasy foreigners think they were dealing with?

It grieved the heart and at the same time lifted the spirit to wander through the blitzed marble halls, the crunch of glass underfoot. Most of the counters were matchwood of course, their place taken by trestle tables and doors propped on wooden boxes. All the chandeliers had been wrecked, splinters of crystal dangling limply on broken chains from the ceiling. The goods on display, despite being bomb-blasted and blackened by the smoke, were still of the usual first-rate quality, and amazingly varied. —Black Mamba snakeskin belts. Piano-shaped fudge in 3 kilo boxes. Platinum "His 'n' Hers" roller skates. "Country Recipe"

110

Cotswold Pizzas. Pearl-inlaid toilet roll holders. Fourteen-piece alligator luggage with matching personalised brolly.

But the most wonderful, heart-warming thing of all was the staff. Pale, twitching, hollow-eyed and battle-scarred, wearing steel helmets stencilled "Harrods" and flak jackets edged with royal blue piping, they were as unfailingly polite and knowledgeable and helpful as ever. A warning siren might sound at any moment (and invariably did), yet they carried on with their appointed duties, bloody but unbowed. They knew at once where to find the nearest Red Cross post, could dress a splinter wound as ably as wrap a parcel or charge to credit, would lead thirty or forty people in community singing during a blackout with stoical aplomb. Indeed, it was strange but true,—and much quoted by the media,—that applications to join the staff had quadrupled since the bombings began; the greater the wreckage and human carnage, the more people flocked to do their bit at this great heart and soul of the nation's indomitable commercial defiance.

Reporters set up a permanent bivouac in Raphael Street in order to interview and photograph survivors on the spot. There was a good deal of competition between the tabloids to sign up victims to an exclusive contract, the most horrendously injured naturally commanding the top prices. "£££s-Per-Stitch" became the bargaining factor, so that a fifty-stitcher, as it was known in the trade, could demand a high fee for an exclusive, while anything over eighty stitches, providing it was face and neck, could ask the earth and get it, with BUPA and three weeks' recuperation in Honduras thrown in. Amputees, especially children, did well, as did pet dogs; poodles, setters and Labradors being the favoured breeds.

Stories went round of people walking up and down Knightsbridge all day long hoping to get caught in the next blast. Some victims were devious, and had been known to extend superficial wounds with concealed razor blades, transforming them from a mere scratch into a lucrative "fifty-stitcher facial".

But, as ever, competition was fierce and getting fiercer. Now the loss of an eye was coming to be regarded as the minimum for a front-page splash. There were those who dreamt of the dream

111

scoop: an eighteen-year-old nubile bride-to-be scarred and blinded (both eyes) while out shopping for her trousseau.

The roof of the building is hazed in smoke from an incendiary device, glimpsed by Vail as the car completes the detour and heads west once more. A news bulletin within the hour will give the names of a dozen or so groups, factions or tendencies squabbling to claim responsibility.

Oddly, the newspaper story has awakened in Vail a sickening unease. Ever since he became rich and famous his resolution to kill somebody has atrophied, and now he feels an unaccustomed stirring of guilt. He is riding high on the hog in his white Merc with his black chauffeur, why rock the boat? He has his yellow card and his Resident Alien permit. He has sufficient fuckable material to last him a lifetime,—more than enough, what with Angie and Virgie and the twenty-three thousand four hundred and seventy-nine members of his fan club.

It is so easy to ignore and forget. In any case, his little girl will have rotted into the ground by now, along with the tartan blanket.

He settles back into the deep moquette and turns to the FT Index. In the mirror his chauffeur's broad black face switches to full beam as he steers the Merc along the Kensington Road.

At the studio in the carpeted, quiet and calm dressing-room Vail changes from dark puce double-breasted blazer, tan Daks slacks and slim patent slip-on shoes into soiled muffler, torn jacket, frayed trousers and laceless ripped pumps.

He has already plastered used diesel oil on his hair, worked grime into his eye-sockets, smeared his cheeks with soot and finished off with a light powdering of coal dust. He nearly forgets his fingernails: scrapes them through a tub of gas-cooker grease and dunks them in fresh dog turd. Per-fect.

The call comes. "VTR in Studio 9," and Vail shuffles off to tape the show in all his glory.

Reliable sources had it that *Bootstraps* had found favour at the most senior executive levels and as a consequence of this the producers of the show,—Bryce Ransom and Virgie Hance,—had been given the green light to extend its run into the indefinite future, which in television terms is thirteen weeks. Everyone was cock o' hoop at the news. Champagne was opened and supped from polystyrene cups. Secretaries were chased into filing rooms and interfered with. Ed Flesh sent a cablegram of congratulation sprinkled liberally with percentages and £ signs. Bryce Ransom voiced the opinion, which seemed to be shared by everyone, that it was, "Super uptight fuck cunts finally it just have didn't to break!"

(Vail has come to the conclusion that he is either talking backwards or in anagrams, but still can't decipher sense or meaning.)

The "philosophy" behind the show, as explained by Virgie Hance to newspaper reporters, is to make cripples get up off their stumps and do something with their lives instead of just lying back on their bed sores begging for sympathy and suppurating and whingeing about it. You had to learn to crap in nests other than your own. It was no good, for instance, patients in terminal cancer wards bemoaning their lot and blaming society; since when had society given them cancer? So why they expect society to feel sorry for them and pick up the tab?

Similarly, Virgie expounded, who was to blame for bringing deformed imbeciles into the world? Certainly not the state. Accidents of nature were God-given, not man-made. Unreasonable, therefore, to look to secular tax-payers to foot the bill for what the Almighty, in all His omnipotent wisdom, had thought fit to decree. Didn't the Church say, "If thy right hand offend thee, cut it off?" The Church didn't say anything about relying on subsidised health care to cut it off for you: the emphasis, surely, was on self-reliance and doing your own dirty work.

One of the most successful shows (ratings-wise) had been the one in which a paraplegic basket case and a thalidomide victim had been encouraged to crawl through a pipe of untreated farm slurry to reach a key that unlocked a casket containing two phials of golden liquid. One was cider, the other urine. The winner of the "race" had the choice of which phial to drink, but once having chosen then had to drink the liquid straight down, even if he discovered he'd picked the wrong one. This led to much gleeful anticipation and hilarity from the studio audience as they breathlessly watched the faces of the two contestants at the moment the phials touched their lips. It was felt (at the most senior executive levels) that this particular show best combined a moral tract with a spot of harmless fun, sugaring the pill of the message as it were.

Another rib-tickling wheeze, dreamt up at one of the weekly programme planning meetings, was to have someone with Parkinson's Disease administer an insulin injection to an aged diabetic already in the final stages of toxic shock coma. Would the old crock get the needle in time,—and in the right place,—or would he end up like a pin cushion before the medics rushed in at the very last moment to save him with "red alert" emergency procedure under the full glare of studio lights and the mesmerised stare of the goggling millions? Here were knockabout farce and tension combined,—laughter one minute, white-knuckled suspense the next,—making the point that, even supposedly suffering from the jitters of Parkinson's Disease, *nobody's* hand shook to such a degree that he couldn't control it when occasion demanded. Although in fact he did miss the vein fourteen times before locating the spot, and then more by accident than design.

Despite being in an off-peak slot the show climbed high in the JICTAR ratings, even outplacing *Feet 'n' Porridge*. It tickled the nation's funny-bone, inspiring a craze for such jokes as: "Where's the first place spastics go when they attend school in the morning?" "Assembly." And "What do spastics do before the school holidays?" "Break up." Saloon bars and hairdressing salons all over the country rocked.

114

Rumours percolated down to the studio to the effect that the show met with the approval of certain people in Govt circles, and that the PM was said to be a keen viewer; supreme accolade indeed.

As a result of this success Vail was invited to meet the Head of Documentaries and Current Affairs, Laine Vere Jumper, an immensely tall aristocratic man with a noble brow and a failing chin, spotted bald head, pink glasses and velvet bow tie, whose drawling speech was out of sync with his lip movements. First came the empty mouthings followed seconds later by the appropriate matching sounds. This gave the impression that at the start of every sentence the unfortunate man was gulping water like a goldfish in a bowl.

Laine Vere Jumper himself never watched TV on principle, though he studied the ratings with a savage analytic eye and heard about the programmes from his secretary, a homely body with a blue rinse by the name of Mrs Stretcher. Mrs Stretcher had no time for arty-farty nonsense; she liked medium two-shots interspersed by profile close-ups, interviewer and interviewee darkening to silhouette against a pale cyclorama as the credits rolled up, and a signature tune you could hum as you went to make the cocoa and put the cat out. Legend in the building had it that Mrs Stretcher could spot a stinkeroo even before the station ident had faded. She thought *Bootstraps* "so true to life" and "hilariously funny without resorting to smut and innuendo". It was the ultimate stamp of approval.

"........ I trust that we're looking after you," Laine Vere Jumper drawls at Vail in his delayed-action voice. They are sitting in his fifteenth-floor executive office suite sipping chilled golden wine from green crystal goblets. One complete wall is all blank television screens while another is all glass, overlooking a London skyline crumbling at the edges from the effects of sulphuric downpours. The hissing of the rain is no longer merely onomatopoeic. "........ You seem to have adjusted remarkably quickly to fame, fortune and success .... Getting plenty of tit and fanny?"

The last three words of this sentence are vibrating the molecules in the air even as Laine Vere Jumper is sipping his wine, which is a cute trick if you can do it. Why, thinks Vail, the dying words of this man could be still ringing in your ears after he had actually expired.

"More than adequate, thank you. Yourself?"

"........ Oh, I'm queer as a coot," Laine Vere Jumper confides. "........ The female form disgusts me .... So verbose .... An abundance of epidermis."

"I'd never thought of it in quite that way before."

"........ You heterosexuals never do .... Leanness and sparsity of form are what appeal to me." He shudders with exquisite distaste and crosses amazingly long tapering legs. "........ I detest grossness however it chooses to manifest itself .... And the world today is too unutterably gross .... One despairs .... Every time I see Selina flashing her pudendum in public I feel positively dire."

"I suppose it is a bit overfacing," Vail has to concede.

"........ And goodness me, tits that size oughtn't to be allowed out of captivity .... Did you know, for instance, Jack, that life on this planet is in danger of being swamped by mammaries? .... My God, they're *everywhere* .... There are probably more tits per hectare than hairs on a navvy's arse .... And I should know .... Imagine, this inordinate plentitude of tit might well signal the end of civilization as we know it."

Laine Vere Jumper seems genuinely distressed at the prospect and takes another sip of piss-coloured wine with eyes painfully screwed tight.

Vail wonders whether all heads of departments in television companies are homosexual, and if so, why there was so much breast and female pudenda filling the screens of the nation night after night. Of course, it takes but a moment's thought to realise that ratings dictated content just as content determined ratings,

116

and therefore there wasn't all that much of a paradox about it after all. Aristocratic homosexual he might be, but Laine Vere Jumper isn't fool enough to deny the great public sufficient sub-Freudian tit with which to smother itself.

[6]

Wayde Dake Ass. Inc. reports in person:

"Howdy," the Texan booms, looming over them like a sandstone cliff and wielding a thick file which he slaps on Vail's ceramic and glass coffee table. "These phone calls. Guy by the name of Tex Rivett. Heard of him?"

Vail shakes his head.

"Sneaky little bastard. Member of a subversive underground cell seeking to overthrow the *status quo*. Arrived in London on August 6 in a milk tanker."

Vail goggles in disbelief and terror.

"Known associates include a guy by the name of Urban Brown and the leader of the cell, Fully Olbin. There's a girl too, but we can't trace an ID on her. Sure you don't know any of these people?"

"Not that I'm aware of."

Angie sets down a tray and they all sip coffee in silence. Vail ponders the remarkable coincidence of two people arriving in London in a milk tanker on the same day. The only other explanation he can think of is that *he* is Tex Rivett, but as he knows he isn't he dismisses it. No wonder there were questions in the House.

"Any idea why they should want to contact you? Money? Blackmail? Drugs?"

"Jack doesn't deal in drugs," Angie says quickly.

"No, Rivett does," Wayde Dake says. "That's how they finance their operation and get people to do them 'favours'. For some reason they must want you."

"What can they possibly want me for?"

"To do them a favour, I guess." The coffee cup is like a thimble

117

in the American's giant sandstone fist. "You can get into places they can't. You meet people they can't get access to."

"Are they dangerous?" Vail asks.

"Extremely. They've been known to kill people who annoyed them, even one teensy-weensy little bit. Sometimes for no reason at all. The person Brown already has a murder-one rap hanging over his head. Strangled and dumped a woman on the A422 outside the wire. But we'll get him or my name's not Weird Ache."

"How do you know it was him?"

"Did it with the belt from his overcoat. Forensic identified his prints."

"On a fabric belt?"

"On her pantihose and undergarments. He interfered with her before, during and after the incident, then snuck through the wire."

"Not in a milk tanker?"

"In the trunk of the limo belonging to the world champion snooker player Steve Davis. Stole some of Steve's gear too, the little rat."

"I hope he was insured."

"Who'd insure terrorist scum like that?"

"I meant Steve."

"Oh sure, Steve was insured, luckily."

Something beeped in Wayde Dake's breast pocket and he leapt up, towering above them like a fissured pillar of rock in Monument Valley, his head very near the ceiling. It was a Priority Z call and he had to leave right away: a person or persons unknown had made a threat against the life and property of the Honourable Guy Naecological, Scottish chairman of the sex shop chain that bore his name.

Vail is quite seriously worried. "What do you think I ought to do?"

"Flesh would like you bugged. Protect his investment."

"How does that work?"

"Simple implant. Minor surgery. Nothing to it. You can hardly see the lump."

"I suppose that means I walk round transmitting signals all day long."

"No problem. Except maybe sometimes you interfere with radio-controlled mini-cabs,—send them to places that don't exist," Wayde Dake tells him. "And providing you don't go near any terrorist devices you have nothing to fear."

"Terrorist devices? Why . . . what happens?"

The massive American wraps his brown hand round Vail's,— "You tend to activate them",—and departs.

[7]

In Room 709 they congregate every Tuesday morning at eleven to plan the following week's programme. Excitement today because Laine Vere Jumper has received a personal appeal from a Govt minister to publicise the Deformed Imbeciles Fund, which is being sponsored by a famous multinational pharmaceuticals corporation whose head office is in Switzerland.

Virgie Hance gives them the lowdown.

"The theme is 'caring sharing', which both the Govt and the drug company are particularly anxious to get across. Our job is to make a selective choice of suitable DIs and feature them in the show."

"Wonderful," somebody enthuses. "Pure JICTAR."

"Schedule tight too fingers out don't we pull," Bryce Ransom reminds everyone sternly, temples throbbing.

(Vail is secretly amazed: he practically understood! Either the producer is becoming more coherent or Vail is adjusting to the lingo.)

"Do they have to crawl through anything?" asks a slender-arsed PA in denims, sharpened pencil poised to stab a note. "Treacle, diesel oil, slurry? We have to order tankers of the stuff weeks in advance."

"I wouldn't personally view that as conducive to attaining the right image portrayal," says the man from the drug company. "The little bastards will induce enough public sympathy as it is."

"Agreed." Virgie Hance smiles at him with her gapped teeth

119

through which smoke writhes as smog through tombstones. "We need basket cases. We're into stumps, boys and girls. Wiggly protuberances in place of fingers. Malformed heads and glassy eyes,—you get the picture. Ideas?"

The director of the show, who enthused earlier, has one. "I could crane-mount a fisheye and dolly in, slice through to a long shot with Jack in the middle of a whole pack of them surrounded by dry ice."

"Blaize," Virgie says wearily. "We're talking concept, not focking execution. You'll get your chance to dazzle. I'm after angles, pegs, hooks. Where do we *find* the little sods for a start?"

"U.M.P.S.?" somebody chimes in from down the table.

Virgie sneaks a frowning glance at Bryce Ransom. "That's under wraps isn't it? No, too sensitive. They've got plenty of DIs, but no. Zilch that."

"I could lay a family on you," Josh Rogan tells the assembly fliply. "Mom, Pop, uncles, aunts, kids."

Virgie's green eyes are alight. "That is brilliant! Really? Are they all DIs, the whole focking shebang?"

"Pop's intact, a pretty straight guy. But the kids are fantastic. 'The legs of the lame are not equal: so is a parable in the mouths of fools.' Proverbs 26, Verse 7. Wait till you eyeball them."

Josh Rogan, the California Baptist, or "CB" as he is known to his friends, has been called in to act as religious adviser to *Bootstraps*. Vail cannot understand how he comes by his tan and sun-bleached hair; the weather has been dour and overcast for weeks past. And why does he speak in a sliding transatlantic jive when he comes from Basingstoke?

The drug company man isn't overtly impressed. He says worriedly, "What kind of deformities exactly? They're not thalidomide, I hope? This is hard PR, remember, not Come To Meek Jesus Week. We don't want any adverse reflection on our long and honourable corporate tradition." He has a widow's peak and glasses like Himmler used to wear and carries perpetual worry and fear on his corrugated brow. He has hairy knuckles and his mouth is as tight as a sutured wound.

120

"No problem," Josh Rogan assures him with his lazy charming smile which illuminates the room like a lighthouse beam. His bleached hair is artfully layered to the nape of his tanned and graceful neck. He is lean and lithe, terrifically attractive and pretends not to be, which compounds the felony. Vail wonders how many souls he has saved. "Congenital interbreeding. I helped obtain for them crutches and walking frames and stuff. 'Lo, children are an heritage of the Lord: and the fruit of the womb is His reward.' Psalms 127, Verse 3. They're cool."

"This clicks, I feel it. Bry, don't you? We do it on film, not studio. Get into gritty actuality. Cut the sentimental crap. Show it as it is, puke and all. Do they live in a tower block? We can fix it, whatever. Give it a Ken Loach feel. Slice to the bone, hit them hard and low, then pitch in with the big sell. It's coming together, I like it, it feels right. Suze, book the O.B. and an eight-man crew. Check make-up and wardrobe. Christ, this is better than a triple orgasm!"

Apparently the family is called the Baths. Given Virgie's enthusiasm no one is prepared to object or disagree, and Bryce Ransom seems happy to go along with it. The director has caught the bug and is busy sketching set-ups on his block of graph paper. The drug company man is making copious notes in a leather-backed book. Virgie is frigging herself under the table. Vail seems to recall that he too once had a family somewhere.

The meeting has drifted away somewhere. Bryce Ransom has gone. The room is quiet except for the slurp of Virgie's fingers. The director says:

"Anybody seen the Bergman retrospective at Camden Screen? Superb minimalism. Stupendous montage."

"I thought she was good in *Casablanca*," Vail agrees, "though I prefer Ava Gardner, who has a bigger chest."

"Say," Josh Rogan says. "How about we use my group for the backing track? I could add some reeds and horns and make the whole thing cool and mellow. Fifties' smoky jazz cellar."

"Uh, I like that," Virgie says with a faint gasp. "Muted Charlie Parker with understated percussion. A bird wailing in the wilderness. It's coming, it's coming, I can feel it . . ."

"We'll have to fly them in from LA," Josh Rogan tells the assembly. His brown hand and long pale fingernails slip inside his V-necked T-shirt to stroke his bronzed chest. "We'll need an arranger, mixer, producer and studio time. Say three weeks minimum."

"Suze will do the fixing. What's the group called?"

"The Joyful Messengers."

Vail is bemused. "I understood you were a preacher?"

"That's right, man."

"But you run a pop group?"

"All God's work," says Josh Rogan reverently. "The message is in the music. We bring joy to the hearts of men. Last year we covered 35,000 miles on three continents doing forty-two gigs."

"'Let every man abide in the same calling wherein he was called.' Corinthians 7, Verse 20." (Vail)

"'Ye see then how that by works a man is justified, and not by faith only.' James 2, Verse 24." (Rogan)

"'It is better to hear the rebuke of the wise, than for a man to hear the song of fools.' Ecclesiastes 7, Verse 5." (Vail)

"'Blow ye the trumpet in Zion, and sound an alarm in my holy mountain: let all the inhabitants of the land tremble: for the day of the Lord cometh, for it is nigh at hand.' Joel 2, Verse 1." (Rogan)

"How do you get the money for all this travelling? I mean, who pays?" Vail asks curiously.

"We pray. The Lord provides."

Looking at Josh Rogan's Californian tan and sun-bleached hair Vail reckons this is a more generous God than he has hitherto allowed for. Praying certainly seems to produce results.

"Additionally we operate our own travel agency, limousine valeting service and record label out of LA,—if you ever need a flight at discount, mention my name."

"Thanks, I will."

"You're welcome."

The drug company man looks worriedly at his watch. "Let's not lose sight of our theme, which is 'caring sharing'. The Fund cares for the DIs, sees to their welfare and so on, but the public has to play its part by sharing the burden. How much are we likely to rake in?"

"Just one second," Vail interjects, puzzled. "I thought your company was sponsoring the scheme?"

"That we are," the worried drug company man avers. "But the appeal will fund it."

"What appeal?"

"The appeal to the public. We show the plight of this family,—the Baths,—ask for charitable donations, and they send them in. The public shares what it has with us."

"Who's 'us'?"

"Well, when I say 'us' I don't mean 'us' *us*, the corporation, if that's what you were thinking. Only a reasonable and fair proportion will come to the corporation for out-of-pocket administrative, advertising, travel and personal expenses and so on. The rest will go towards caring for the DIs, paying for medication, prosthetics, artificial limbs and the like. It's really very straightforward."

"What exactly are you doing by way of sponsorship then?" Vail asks, feeling stupid, feeling he has missed something.

"Lending our name, our prestige, our goodwill," the worried man from the drug company informs him. "For a small consideration. After all, this is a Govt initiative; you can't expect a commercial enterprise to pick up the tab. The fact that certain Cabinet Ministers have shares in the corporation is neither here nor there, let's get that clear. This is straight-down-the-middle altruism on our and the Govt's part."

"Good, that's settled, that's out of the way," Virgie says firmly. "How many in this so-called family?" she asks, turning to the California Baptist.

"Eight. Father,—he's the normal one,—Granny Bertha and Auntie Beatrice; Uncle Forster, he's in his late twenties and is really the brother of seventeen-year-old Rita who everyone calls Reet; Vic, nineteen or twenty, vicious and bored; Dumpy, she's twelve; and Little Com, who's of indeterminate age and sex."

"No mother?"

"She ran off with a big black man."

"How big?" Virgie asks with a little catch of breath. "Huge?" Josh Rogan shrugs indifferently. "I never met him."

The drug company man is not happy; he is distinctly worried. "They sound pretty average to me. Father, granny, uncles, aunts, kids of indeterminate age and sex. We're talking real deformity here, or at any rate that was my impression. I mean, are these people just regular oddballs, mental defectives or what?"

"He has a point," Virgie says to Josh Rogan. "Crutches and walking frames are all very well but they don't make for good television. We need harrowing scenes that bring a lump to the throat and a hand to the wallet. Are the Baths really primetime we have to ask ourselves?"

"Relax. They'll freak you out. Really. Trust Forte."

"What do you think, Jack?" Virgie says.

"What about?"

"Well . . . about all this . . . you know . . . this . . ."

"The table? Looks all right to me. Smooth veneer, nice shine."

"The show. What do you think about the show?"

"Fine. Wonderful. Couldn't be better. So far so good."

"Suppose I pan to some rusty railings and do a slow dissolve into the little kid's face. —Has it got a face?" the director asks Josh Rogan. "Great! Then pull back to a two-shot in its mother's arms,—"

"Haven't you been listening, dumbo, the mother ran off!" Virgie Hance hisses.

"Granny's wizened arms, that's even better. Dolly in to the gnarled arthritic hands clutching the kid and go into soft focus . . ."

No one is paying heed to this mumbo-jumbo. Virgie Hance is dwelling languorously on the physical attributes of large black men. The drug company man is calculating his expenses and worrying about the hair he keeps finding on the pillow every morning. Josh Rogan is checking airline timetables and mulling over II Samuel Chapter 3 Verse 7. Suze, the slender-arsed PA, isn't thinking about anything in particular, except perhaps her I Ching forecast for the coming week. As for our hero, he's misplaced his daughter's name and can't for the life of him find it.

[8]

[Up to this point Vail has not acted so much as been acted upon. This is understandable, given his traumatic circumstances. He has been swept along by events, been content to be, because he could not see what else he could do. What sustained him in the early days following his arrival in the capital was an unformed desire to take some kind of action, to take negative and not positive action, and for a while this desire remained comatose, traumatised, undirected, until the moment outside the electrical retailer's when he saw the face on the screen repeated twenty-two times and the unformed desire hardened into focus and resolved itself into a cold deadly ambition (not hate,—nothing so fine and noble as hate) which gave him direction and a kind of iron-tasting nihilistic hope for the future. So even though these events may have seemed arbitrary at the time and Vail a man without motive and purpose, inwardly he had set his mind, his heart and soul on the attainment of a goal that, fantastic as it might have been, was to him practicable and achievable, given time and the random sway of circumstances and events. Because, unlike so many others who have given up the ghost, Vail still had, and has, a touching faith in the ordered mechanism of the universe, in the balance of forces, in the opposing poles of the electromagnetosphere which impose order onto chaos and decree that for every atom of darkness there shall be a photon of light and for every particle its anti-matter equivalent; in other words those immutable laws without which there would be no paper, no pen, and no hand to set down these words, and no one to read them. What has happened is that he has become confused and non-directional in his aspirations, or rather, in

125

his lack of them. He had quite made up his mind to kill, because killing seemed obvious and natural and right (reinstating the ordered mechanism, restoring the balance of forces, etc) and he had no moral qualms about the act because morals are man-made and not God-given. (Even though, perversely, he does not believe in a god, or "God", as such.) The act was to be one of reinstatement and restoration, simply that, which explains why he was not even angry or rageful or motivated by hate, nor even revenge. (Though it could be argued that revenge is concomitant to the perfect order of the universe, balancing the equation, —so to speak, —equilibrating one powerful emotion with another of opposing yet equal strength. For if the desire for revenge didn't exist there would be a void, and as we all know nature abhors a vacuum.) Then time and distance and atrophy set in, and worse, corrosion of the spirit, so that he became merely a plaything of shallow sensation, a water insect skittering over the skin of bogus reality, and almost, but not quite, forgot his cold rageless purpose. Soft cushions and a full belly make us all forget, so we must forgive Vail his weakening of resolve, particularly as he has an excess of nubile women, a white Merc, and a continual stroking of the ego, beneficial as a hot scented bath into which one slides with smirking lassitude. But now fear has entered into the equation, and fear is like a white-hot needle inserted into the anus. What is he afraid of? Like everyone, of being found out. Of not "coming up to the mark". Without being told, or having to be told, he knows full well that he has failed to live up to that commitment which resolved itself while watching the twenty-two selfsame images on the television screens in the electrical retailer's window. (There is, too, the lesser fear of receiving mysterious telephone calls from a terrorist cell, but this has simply triggered the larger, latent fear of his own inadequacy, paltriness of spirit and shortness of memory.) What has happened, he now realises, is that in crossing the wire he has also crossed over into Dremeland, a place where everyone has sunk, some knowingly, some unwittingly, into a light pleasant doze, cosily insular and protected. The frenetic activity in Oxford Street fools no one: they are asleep too, deeply asleep, mere jerky somnambulists buying stuff to pad their dreams with. By voluntary consent

126

everyone is living a daily game of Feet 'n' Porridge, *and the more empty and shrill the laughter the more content they are. And yet, and yet, this Dremeland is a terrifying place, and the sleepwalkers feel it in their bones and nightmares and know it in their heart of hearts. This is one reason for the ceaseless activity: keep moving and the surface tension of Dremeland will support you: stop for even one brief marginal second and you will sink down and down into unfathomable, unimaginable, murky depths. No wonder they skitter! There are charms and spells and incantations to prevent this disastrous sinking, such as the constant repetition of the leader's name, which obviates all necessity to think and wards off attacks of the heeby-jeebies. Thus in times of doubt (dangerous!) you chant until stupefied the same two syllables of iron-clad certitude. Yet another method is a wanton suspension of disbelief, widely used and very popular, in which your natural incredulity is blighted, annulled, indeed stopped dead in its tracks by the sheer breathtaking effrontery of naked, blatant lies. But these, it should be added, are very clever lies, cunningly designed to seduce and take advantage of those base impulses that lurk inside all of us. The lies whisper,—or do they thunder?—that to be kind you have first to be cruel, that to protect the weak you have to be repressive, that to show compassion you have first to demonstrate brute strength, and, above all, that by helping yourself you are, by some impenetrable, convoluted piece of schlock logic, helping others. It is a superb philosophy because it enables you to indulge in soft cushions and a full belly to your heart's content while at the same time salving your conscience (or the flabbily dormant faculty which passes for such) as you skitter merrily along on the surface tension of your own wilful ignorance, blindness and callous stupidity. But those depths,—my God, those depths!—are but the thickness of a millimetre away! Poke one toe beneath, break that surface tension, and Dremeland will shimmer and fragment and vanish before your eyes. It is not built on rock, not even on shifting sand, but on the illusory premise of enlightened self-interest, a concept so flimsily ramshackle that no one, not even monetarists, dares scrutinise it for fear that both it and they will turn out to be self-evidently non-existent. As for Vail, instinct rather than intellect has*

127

convinced him of much of the above, so that in his bones and nightmares and heart of hearts he knows what he must do; yet the wearing of silk socks and Gucci shoes has immured his toes to the touch and feel of the surface tension and prevented him, even had he wanted to, from penetrating it. That and the endless and readily available supply of women who yearn to have their nipples sucked by a pair of famous lips and to become conjoined, however briefly, to a media personality. And when all is said and done, who can blame him? His bread is buttered both sides and there is ample jam today in Dremeland for everyone.]

[9]

Somehow (Virgie Hance had issued a press release) the newspapers had got wind of the location shoot at the Baths and there was a mêlée of reporters waiting as the cavalcade of trucks, vans, generators and Range Rovers arrived at the door. The house was large and gloomy with crumbling brickwork and a patch of sooty garden at the front. The day was cold and wet, the crew wrapped in waffle-weave thermal underwear, orange parkas and moon boots. So far so good.

Virgie Hance answers the reporters' questions and the director sets up his first shot of the house exterior as Vail sits in the back of the Range Rover sipping coffee laced with brandy from a silver hip flask. Small children with noses dribbling mucus like white candlewax watch him through the window with eyes glassily bright from smack. The area is a social worker's paradise.

A narrow wind blows down the street, rattling the rusted bonnets of cars. It carries with it the whiff of sulphur.

A reporter wants to know what kind of wizard jape Mzzz Hance has in mind for the Baths. Virgie winks: wait and see. Another would like to interview the presenter of the show, but Virgie says that Mr Vail is resting and cannot be disturbed. "UNAVAILABLE VAIL" trumpet the headlines the next day, and "ALL TO KNOW AVAIL" alongside a picture of a group of

128

studiously disconsolate photographers standing in the steaming drizzle. Smart cookies, these newshounds.

Presently Vail's presence is required and he does his piece to camera with the taciturn house as a backdrop. The windows reveal nothing except grimy torn curtains, and in the blasted heath of garden a pram with a ripped hood and buckled wheels lies on its side, the creamy padded interior invaded by green mould. Parts of what appear to be the chassis of a car lean against the wall. There is a broken oil sump filled with water, a swirling film of rainbows shivering on its surface.

The introductory piece to camera in the can, the crew break for coffee and hot bacon sandwiches. The director confers with Virgie and together they go over the shooting script they have drawn up. Vail has had no hand in this; he is a minion, an appendage, is content to be so, and sits in the back of the Range Rover snuffled down in a bulky suede jacket thickly lined with lambswool which covers his telly costume of rags and tatters. The faces of the urchins press against the glass, leaving smears and bits of glutinous matter. He wonders why they aren't in school. Schools are still open, aren't they? Or if not in school, surely there must be an amusement arcade at the end of the street, or a video shop? He doesn't like being recognised, it makes him feel exposed and vulnerable, and he resents them for it. It's as if they've peeled him down to raw goosepimpled chicken skin. That and the irritating ticking sensation in his groin combine to make a dull flare of anger rise up in him and he calls the unit manager to clear them off.

The street reminds him of hell: the drizzle is eating the brickwork.

After a while the director calls them together and they move inside the house *en masse*. The researcher has been there since daybreak, preparing the Baths for their ordeal by celluloid. As might be expected, the house stinks to high heaven. The rooms are unheated, with little furniture except for twenty-six-inch colour television, video recorder, rack stereo, and Atari games console with thirty cartridges stacked on top. There are mattresses on the floor in most of the rooms and heaps of mildewed clothing. Damp and decay have taken a stranglehold. Virgie doesn't think there's enough debris and orders the researcher to scatter some empty tins, crumpled cornflakes packets, Durex sheaths, margarine tubs and the like. "Jesus, you've seen enough focking television drama to know what it *ought* to look like," she lashes him. "Make it look *real*. Let's get some actuality into this, prick face."

Father is six-feet-seven-inches tall and built like a brick shithouse, with black greasy hair and sideburns that meet under his chin. His staring accusing eyes are of different colours. The index and middle fingers of his left hand are missing up to the second joint and the loose skin has been pulled over the ends and stitched with all the finesse of a butcher tacking a leg of lamb. Nobody has the raw nerve to look him in the eye, except Virgie, to whom he appears as an outsize extra in her private mad vision. She could out-stare Beelzebub providing a 16mm camera and sound boom were to hand.

She asks him where the rest of the family are and instead of replying Father asks her about the money. He wants a facility fee up front and guaranteed overseas residuals; dramatic and cold print rights are reserved but negotiable. Virgie placates him by saying that it's all taken care of and that he has nothing to worry about. And as a measure of goodwill slips him a litre of White Horse. A slow wink hints that he could be in line for something of a more intimate nature if he plays his cards right.

After a tot of brandy to warm them up the crew start filming in earnest. The director's plan is to show members of the family greeting the new day in their own individual ways. He films Granny Bertha awakening from wrinkled sleep and crawling out from her piece of sacking; Reet on the lavatory while Father does his ablutions; Auntie Beatrice putting her teeth in and humming a tuneless melody while she rummages in a cardboard box for something to wear. Next he moves to a set-up in the tiny kitchen with Granny Bertha and Auntie Beatrice preparing "breakfast". As breakfast isn't normally eaten by the Baths as a collective enterprise but carried out on separate mattresses with whatever is available that day, Granny Bertha and Auntie Beatrice have to be prompted step by step, the director calling the moves by numbers.

Granny Bertha is in possession of her mental faculties but is infirm and dithery, while Auntie Beatrice is vacant and forgetful, in the incipient stages of senile dementia. The "breakfast" they finally prepare comprises two bowls of cold rice pudding, gravy granules (mistaken for instant coffee) made in the teapot with tepid water, some fragments of cream crackers in an upturned saucepan lid, six slices of bread as stiff as and the colour of cardboard, an empty jar of marmalade with something living in it, a packet of ravioli left over from a shoplifting expedition, and a lemonade bottle without a label containing Sandoz bleach.

The director wants an "establishing family scene", an "assembly of disparate discrete elements coming together in friendship and communion at the birth of a new day, rather in the manner of Buñuel". Virgie tells him to cut the arty crap and not to be such a focking wanker.

One by one the remainder of the family appears, roused by Father already reeking of whisky fumes with the steel-capped toe of his boot.

Rita or "Reet" is the seventeen-year-old love-child of Father and his sister, Auntie Beatrice. She is tall and spindly and pale as a living ghost, a semi-imbecile with bowed shoulders and a mouth overflowing with buck teeth taking up the entire lower half of her face, the moist bottom lip hanging below the level of her chin. Her hair is tight and frizzy and she wears large spectacles with clear frames which magnify her bulbous eyes to monstrous size. Not a pretty specimen.

She enters the kitchen slowly and silently and sits, upon Granny Bertha's instruction, at the table, head lolling from side to side. When asked by the director what she normally does at this hour of the morning, Reet just grins and dribbles.

Here comes Uncle Forster. Twenty-nine and Reet's quarter-brother, he has squinting suspicious eyes, a concave chest superseded by a pot belly like a concealed dumpling under his pullover, bites his nails and smokes incessantly. Uncle Forster is

131

the arch-criminal of the family, having done time in Risley, Strangeways and Pentonville.

Dumpy and Little Com arrive together, one dragging, the other screaming. As her pet name indicates, Dumpy is a sullen thirteen-year-old with a thick fringe and a pasty complexion who stares fixedly into space and is incapable of uttering a sentence of more than three words which doesn't contain a blasphemy or four-letter epithet. Little Com, the youngest of the tribe, of indeterminate age and sex, is a whining screaming uncontrollable bundle of animal aggression. He/she is never still for long enough to discern any distinguishing marks or features, so it is impossible to say what Little Com actually looks like, except that he/she is bald, yellow and blind. This brings the director close to despair. He can't hold him/her in shot for more than three seconds, and in the final cut Little Com appears as a yellow blur of destructive quantum energy.

The last member of the family, Vic, doesn't materialise. An undernourished nineteen or twenty, with a wispy moustache and fledgling beard and bad teeth, his chief characteristics are that he is vicious and bored. Vic is the father of the child of indeterminate age and sex, by his own mother, though no one in the family would dare admit to it; the child and everyone else regarded Father as its father and referred to him as such, with Vic a spurious "uncle" or "step-brother" or something. It was acknowledged but unspoken that Vic had committed some ghastly act in the past and was quite likely to do it again if provoked.

Little Com's screaming continues unceasingly throughout "breakfast", driving the director insane. The cameraman is spattered with rice pudding. The sound recordist can't hear anything because Auntie Beatrice has absently poured cold gravy from the teapot into the microphone. Reet rocks to and fro, smiling gently with wet teeth, saliva leaking from her lower lip. Uncle Forster leans against the sink, squinting morosely and pugnaciously, legs crossed, folded arms resting on the round dumpling of his belly.

A row of grimy grinning faces is propped on the window sill, noses squelched against the glass, mouthing hysterical obscenities. In the backyard murky flaccid washing hangs on the drooping line like prisoners in a Uruguayan death cell. (So far so good.)

"Where's your focking 'dissolve through soft focus to granny's wizened arms' now?" Virgie yells at the director. "Are you getting any of this, Buñuel, you jerkoff?"

The scene changes.

Vail has been surplus to requirements thus far but is now called upon to "interview" some of the family. Presumably the show has a theme, some underlying purpose, but he can't for the life of him bring it to mind. Is this how television documentaries are made? What, out of all this unmitigated mess and squalor, can there possibly be worth showing to the great British public? And to what end?

The interviews, conducted in the first floor front bedroom, with pee-sodden mattresses on the bare floor, don't go well.

Reet dribbles foolishly into the camera lens, her glasses flaring light. She is a happy, gentle soul, not of this world. The boys in the neighbourhood interfere with her frequently and but for the grace of God and the vigilance of Granny Bertha she would have become pregnant several times over.

"Is it true," Vail asks her, reading from the prepared questions given to him by Virgie Hance, "that if it wasn't for the products of large multinational pharmaceuticals companies you wouldn't be with us today?" (He raises his eyebrows at Virgie in silent plea, who nods emphatically.)

"Hee-yeee-heee-urrghhh-gurghhh-grhhh-heee-yeee-"

(With vigorous signals and mouthings Virgie indicates that Vail is to continue with the next question.)

"So you would definitely say then that but for the miracle of modern drugs you'd be incapable of leading a normal life?"

"Hee-yeee-heee-urrghhh-gurghhh-grrhhh-heee-yeee."

"We can all say that, I suppose."

"Grrhhyeee-(dribble-suck-dribble)-yeee-heee-heee-heee."

"I'm sure ninety-nine per cent of the population would echo that."

133

Reet rocks forward, the bottom half of her face agape and dripping saliva, and touches Vail very gently as if he might break.

"Now now now," says Granny Bertha. "Don't molest the gentleman. He's from the television."

The crew break for tea, coffee, brandy, toast and hot sausage rolls provided by Suze. The talk is of yachts, house extensions, VAT returns, BUPA, and the competing merits of holiday homes in Scotland and the Cotswolds and time-sharing villas in the Algarve. One of the crew kindly gives half a chocolate biscuit to Reet, who sits munching it with intense dedication, chocolate adhering to her front teeth. Auntie Beatrice, whom Granny Bertha must keep in her sight at all times, absent-mindedly lifts her leg and releases a soft rippling fart, smiling beatifically with pleasure.

From below comes Little Com's persistent screeching wail and Dumpy's tirade of foul-mouthed abuse. The researcher, left in charge, is at his wit's end: Dumpy keeps taunting him with a flash of her mucky drawers and none-too-subtle sexual innuendo, which disgusts him (he comes of an upper-class Anglo-Irish family and went to Marlborough) but which incites the grubby watchers at the kitchen window to a frenzy of lewd and lustful gesticulation.

"Where are the *stumps*?" the director complains querulously to Virgie Hance. "And why isn't the Religious Adviser here? How can I make a decent film when I don't have the material? I need *actuality* and you're not giving it to me!"

Virgie agrees. "We'll have to think of something. Jack, any ideas?"

Vail says without thinking, "Why not take them to Tesco's and give them £100 to spend."

"Wonderful!"

"Mightn't that cause mayhem?" the director frowns.

"Yes!" Virgie is scribbling on a pad, flared nostrils billowing smoke.

The director gets the drift and catches alight. "I could shoot them through the wire mesh of a trolley at floor level. Sort of concentration camp feel. Bounce floods of light around. Spare, austere, clinical."

134

"Where is Josh by the way?" Vail inquires.

Virgie says, "Flew back to LA last night. He's cutting an album."

"He doesn't seem to do much preaching."

"No, but he prays a lot."

"You know, this Tesco shoot isn't going to generate much sympathy for the Baths," the director says on reflection. "I thought the object of the exercise was to garner public support for the DI Fund. And what about our 'caring sharing' theme?"

"Use your brain, diarrhoea-face. What better way to touch the heartstrings and whip up sympathy than to see this couple of old crones here with their arms full of products and tears coursing down their flaking sunken cheeks? Or Dumpy and Little Com cramming their faces with all kinds of confectionery they've hitherto only dreamt of or seen on the telly? Reet trying on a cross-your-heart bra and pampering herself with lipstick and powder and dreaming of a beau? Father standing there stunned and emotional at the sight of his family enjoying all the things he's been unable, through force of circumstance, to provide for them? And Uncle Forster and Vic . . ."

But here even Virgie's inspiration, when confronted by a pot-bellied petty crook and a vicious teenage hoodlum, peters out. What to do about Vic and Uncle Forster? Put them in a wheelchair and walking frame? She says briskly, "We'll shoot round them. In any case we can leave them on the cutting-room floor."

"You could make them the heavies of the piece," Vail suggests (a phrase he has heard Angie use).

"*Brilliant!*" chorus Virgie and the director. "We can work in incest and child abuse," Virgie adds, smiling with all her shark's teeth.

"It's a great dramatic counterpoint," the director agrees. "Love, hate, crime and sexual perversion in a London slum-dwelling family. It's got to be a BAFTA nomination. Felliniesque."

There is a crash of splintering timber and Father staggers in, his thumb and two good fingers wrapped around the neck of the whisky bottle. He is in a rare fighting mood, ready to take on all-comers. "Get this," Virgie hisses at the cameraman.

135

Wails from below as Dumpy smashes Little Com over the head with the teapot. The nerve-shattered researcher has fled to the sanctuary of the front room where he finds Uncle Forster slumped on a couch watching a Selina Southorn movie on video. Vic has yet to put in an appearance.

The crew have retreated to the corner of the room as Father threshes about indiscriminately with the whisky bottle. His lank greasy hair hangs in front of his staring-mad bloodshot odd-coloured eyes.

"M' lil gurl," he mumbles incoherently, collapsing onto the mattress and smothering Reet in a clumsy embrace with his heavy tattooed arm.

"Heee-ggreee-grrughh-heee-yeee."

Granny Bertha tries to intercede but her aged limbs are incapable; she pushes Auntie Beatrice forward instead.

"Stop him, stop him! He said never again. He wouldn't. He's your son or brother, stop him!"

"The 11.42 is delayed because of a derailment at Harlow," Auntie Beatrice replies, who was once a station announcer at Liverpool Street. She tugs at her wrinkled stockings. "Tell Norman he needn't bother. We'll collect the fish later if Emily doesn't mind."

Father has his hand under Reet's dress. "Get Uncle Forster. Tell Vic," Granny Bertha shrills at everyone and no one. "He's at it again. He promised he wouldn't, the swine."

"I'm out of stock," the cameraman reports from his crouched position, unclipping the reel.

"Oh fock." Virgie stamps on her cigarette. "Okay, it's a wrap. Now much have we got?"

The cameraman hands the camera to his assistant. "Two thousand feet, five hundred mute."

"We'll break for lunch. Do a set-up in Tesco's in,—" she checks her watch,—"two hours. Holy Mother, do I need a drink."

Virgie, Vail, Suze, the director and crew make their departure leaving Father and Reet on the mattress and Granny Bertha standing impotently over them with gnarled fists and Auntie Beatrice swaying back and forth with a bittersweet smile to the

136

inaudible strains of *I'd Rather be a Beggar with You* sung by Al Bowlly. Downstairs the grinning lecherous urchins have broken into the kitchen and are taking turns at Dumpy over the gas stove while Little Com, a nasty purple bruise on his/her bald yellow head, is strapped to a chair yelling blue murder.

[10]

Vail, in bed in Lord Napier Place, Upper Mall, with Virgie Hance, is having difficulty in rising to the occasion. He is lying naked on Virgie's black silk sheets and she is toiling over him like a Trojan,—long straggling red hair whipping her snow-white freckled shoulders,—in sweating frenzied effort while her breasts slosh and swing about above him like a pair of prolapsed eyeballs hanging out of their sockets.

"Come on, you bastard, come on!" she grates at him from the corner of her mouth, scattering cigarette ash into his eyes and hair. "Make it stiff, you horny swine!" and other similar implorations, all to no avail.

This is rather strange, to Vail as much as to anyone, because not forty minutes earlier, during a recording of *Bootstraps* in Studio 9, Virgie had scuttled on all fours over the tangle of cables, crawled underneath the desk at which Vail was sitting reading from autocue and, while ostensibly whispering script changes to him, had unzipped his flies and given him head.

Vail's performance on camera, as observed by those in the control box, had been his best so far. The director had clapped his hands and Suze had to keep moistening dry lips. The climax of the show had happily coincided with Vail's personal climax, as was evident from the thrusting incisiveness of his delivery and the shining zeal in his eyes. Afterwards, while Virgie wiped her chin, the entire studio broke into spontaneous applause.

It was a "wonderful" show and a "tremendous performance" on Vail's part, as Mrs Stretcher, watching on a monitor, later reported to Laine Vere Jumper.

Still hot and rabid and lusting for more, Virgie had bundled Vail into the car and ordered the chauffeur to put his foot down and stop for nothing and no one, which nearly resulted in a nasty accident as the Merc took the entrance lane on the way out and narrowly missed a car coming in, driven by Anthony Quayle, the world famous and much-respected actor, who was arriving to do a voice-over for a travel documentary.

Luckily for Vail, Virgie and Mr Quayle, the black chauffeur was an expert driver and took evasive action by mounting the central reservation and demolishing a directional bollard.

Once in the flat they got straight down to it, a tumbling, giggling, squealing mass of flesh and limbs as they tore off their own and each other's clothing. At this point Vail was still fairly eager, had sufficiently recovered his virility, so he thought, to put up a creditable performance, and indeed was quite looking forward to it.

But. Now. Virgie slumps back exhausted after pumping away at nothing for ten minutes, disappointed and hurt, grinding her gapped teeth in frustration. She lights a fresh cigarette from the one smouldering in the corner of her mouth and sucks in a revivifying lungful. There is silence except for the wheezing of her chest.

Vail slumps too, staring at the ceiling. There is a faint but persistent tingling sensation in his groin, like the buzzing of an electrical current. He wonders if Virgie's incessant pounding and grinding has broken something, and gently probes the turkey's gizzard containing his testes.

"Jesus, you're not *playing* with yourself, I hope!" Virgie retorts, rounding on him angrily, cigarette dangling from the corner of her mouth, eyes screwed up against the writhing worm of smoke. "Don't tell me you'd rather wank than screw, you working-class jerkoff!"

"I think you might have damaged my equipment, that's all."

She leans over his nether quarters, mouth gaping aslant to suck in air, and cups him in her hand. Vail recoils as the burning tip of the cigarette, carelessly and unheedingly stuck between her lips, hovers within inches of his flaccid, defenceless manhood.

138

She weighs him in her palm, frowning, and it is Virgie and not Vail who stiffens.

"Holy Mother shit!"

"What,—?"

"You've got three balls."

"No, just the regulation two."

"I can feel three."

"Two are mine, the third is an implant. Wayde Dake's idea. Or rather, Ed Flesh's. He thought that I ought to be bugged for my own protection."

"You've got a bug in your balls?" Virgie says in a tone of quiet stupefaction.

"It's out of the way; normally I never notice it."

"You mean to say they're monitoring this? Some guy is sitting in a darkened room somewhere wearing headphones listening to this and taping the sounds my cunt makes on his focking machine?"

"I don't think it's that sort of bug. According to Wayde it sends out pulsed signals so that they know where to find me any time day or night. Your secret's safe with me."

At this, however, Virgie seems somewhat downcast. The possibility that her intimate body sounds are being recorded for posterity has caused the muscles in her vaginal walls to contract and fluid to be secreted in copious amounts.

With her fingertips she feels the implant in its pulpy sac and speaks to it: "Testing, testing, testing. One two three. The quick brown fox jumps over the lazy hen. Over."

"You won't get a reply."

"Not even if I extend the antenna?" Virgie says craftily.

"You're welcome to try," Vail says, lying back submissively, a smile burgeoning on his lips.

[11]

Vail's car and chauffeur are waiting in the cold dead street as he leaves Lord Napier Place, Upper Mall, at three in the morning.

The chauffeur grins, as one male to another, and says, "How'd it go, bawz? You boogie on down wid dat chick?"

Vail nods wearily and sinks back into the moquette. He has, so he believes, aquitted himself manfully, but at considerable cost to his psychic reserves of equilibrium and wellbeing: he is a man on a knife-edge, balanced precariously between, on the one side, the headlong rush of exotic events, happenings and circumstances, and on the other, the total black emptiness of failure of nerve and lack of resolve. The trouble with being seduced, he has found, is that it's so seductive.

The car glides off through the quiescent city taking a tired Vail not, as he thinks, back to his flat, but to a secret destination somewhere south of the river; and the big black chauffeur, hired to protect him, is in fact none other than the leader of a terrorist cell by the name of Fully Olbin.

The plot thickens.

When Vail opens his eyes (the ride having lulled him into a gentle doze) he discovers that the car has stopped in a mean little street hemmed in by derelict warehouses. A boat toots nearby, but otherwise all is peaceful and silent as the grave. The tall slablike empty-eyed warehouses shut out the night, rising, so it seems, endlessly into the sky. They,—Vail, Fully Olbin,—might be in a tunnel, or in a groove cut deep into the earth, such is their isolation from the rest of sleeping London.

"What are we doing here?" Vail naturally wants to know, having expected the flat, a nightcap, and the soft ocean of bed.

Fully Olbin's split-melon grin has gone, along with his Uncle Tom patois. "There's a score to be settled, a debt to be paid, Jack," he informs Vail in a brisk, matter-of-fact manner. "Follow me. Any funny business and I'll break your toothcaps."

Vail sensibly does as he's told and enters the building behind Fully Olbin, who bolts the door behind them. There is a smell of wet newspaper. They climb umpteen flights of echoing stairs in

140

the darkness and come finally to a long dusty room that takes up the whole of one floor. Fully Olbin leads the way across floorboards worn smooth by generations of porters, warped and soft and dangerously rotten in places, to a meat locker in the corner, the size of a room in itself. He swings open the heavy thick door and gestures Vail inside. Vail enters, feeling something click in his groin, and is confronted by two men, or rather one man and a boy or youth, sitting on packing cases at a table fashioned out of more packing cases. The man is Urban Brown and the boy or youth Vail recognises as the boy or youth from the Sandbach stat who gave him the *Temporal* in exchange for a favour not yet, he recalls with a sudden sickly feeling, discharged.

The door thumps solidly shut and Fully Olbin works the long iron handle to seal it. Even the silence outside cannot penetrate. The walls and ceiling consist of dull leaden-looking sheets of metal riveted together as in a ship's hull. There is a single caged wall light and several rows of metal bars fastened by struts to the ceiling, S-shaped meat hooks with sharpened ends hanging from them.

"Guess what," the boy or youth says. "I've been trying to ring you." His grimy torn T-shirt reads: *Smash the Blood-Sucking NHS*. His hair lies lankly on his shoulders.

"That was you was it?" Vail says lightly with a grin, hoping to make conversation. He tries not to notice a large area of dried blood on the floor with hair stuck to it. "You must be Tex Rivett."

"Right first time," the boy or youth says, grinning with mildewed teeth.

"Sit down, Jack," Fully Olbin says.

"After you."

"No, I'll stand. You sit."

Vail sits. His balls are aching. That damn Virgie Hance had very nearly ripped them off.

"You must have been expecting something like this, Jack," says Fully Olbin, stripping off his black gloves to reveal his black hands and large pale fingernails.

"Something like what?" Vail asks, blinking a little.

"You owe us one, don't you?" Fully Olbin says, massive in his chauffeur's neatly-buttoned grey uniform, gloves clasped in both huge hands at his groin, booted legs straddled apart on the bloodstained floor. "Remember?"

"Why yes of course I do. I was just waiting for you to make contact. You know, get in touch. He,—Tex,—said you would sooner or later. Yes you could say I was expecting something like this, yes."

"We've been waiting for the right moment. And this is it. Now we can move. Now that you're where we wanted you to be, we can act. That's why we waited, bided our time."

"I see." Vail frowns. "Where exactly am I that you wanted me to be?"

"Right where you are, Jack. Rich, famous and successful. You'd be no good to us otherwise, would you?"

"I guess not. What do you mean, 'good' to you?"

"I mean in a position to do us some good. You can help us achieve our objective."

"Which is?"

"To overthrow the *status quo*. You know that already. Wayde Dake told you that when he presented the report on Tex, Brown and me."

Vail remembers, and the memory niggles at him.

He says, looking round, "So this is what a terrorist cell looks like. I've often wondered. Tell me, why meet here, inside a meat locker?"

"Haven't you noticed, squire?" Tex Rivett says with his green grin. "It's lead-lined. Get it?"

"No," Vail says, shaking his head. "Sorry?"

"The signals from that bug you're carrying can't transmit from here. They're blocked. Neat, eh?"

Vail experiences a shiver of apprehension. But then what, he reasons, would his death achieve? No, they didn't intend to kill him, because then how could he help them achieve their objective of overthrowing the *status quo*? Unless his death was an integral

142

part of the plan. But then how would the murder of a media personality do them the "good" that Fully Olbin had spoken of? What "good" could come of that?

Fully Olbin says, "Have you ever heard of the U.M.P.S. Programme?"

"No, I've never watched it."

"You've never discussed it in production meetings at Thames with Bryce Ransom and Virgie Hance?"

"No."

Fully Olbin unbuttons the front of his tunic and pulls out a large manilla envelope into which he inserts his large black hand and withdraws a sheaf of photographs secured by a metal spring clip. He opens the clip and presents the first photograph for Vail's inspection. It is captioned *U.M.P.S. Programme: Phase One* and shows a bulldozer pushing some metal drums into a hole in the ground under floodlights. The driver of the bulldozer is encased in a white polystyrene suit, wears goggles and a mask and rubber gauntlets up to the elbows.

The second photograph shows the same area in daylight after the bulldozer has filled in the hole and levelled out the ground. Workmen, similarly encased in white protective coveralls, are planting saplings supported by staves driven into the raw tracked earth. In the background, perhaps two hundred metres from the site, is a children's playground with swings, slide and climbing frame, and beyond that five high-rise flats blocking out the horizon.

Fully Olbin hands him the next, third, photograph, captioned *U.M.P.S. Programme: Phase Two*. This shows protective-suited workmen piping liquid from an unmarked grey tanker into a stream. The stream bubbles and froths and yellowish steam rises up through which can be seen a two-storey building with many windows. The next, fourth, photograph is taken from the same vantage point only now the tanker has gone and children are playing in the asphalt yard of the school.

143

Another photograph,—*U.M.P.S. Programme: Phase Three*,—is of a long waiting-room filled to bursting point with upwards of two hundred people. In the foreground a harassed-looking nurse is reading out names from a clipboard, and next to her stands an Indian doctor caught in the act of yawning and rubbing his left eye. The people on the benches are gaunt-faced, haggard, hopelessness exuding from every pore.

In the next photograph the same Indian doctor is examining a child whose face is blotchily red with raw weeping sores. The child, a girl of about ten, has bare patches where her scalp shows through. Vail passes quickly over this one, hardly bearing to look.

Without a word Fully Olbin hands him a photograph captioned *U.M.P.S. Programme: Phase Four*. This one portrays a naked middle-aged woman strapped to a metal table with two laboratory technicians in green gowns and masks leaning over her holding stainless steel instruments: one technician has clamped her mouth open to its fullest extent while the other pokes and probes far down her throat, his hand practically inside her mouth.

The next photograph is of a similar laboratory scene in which a child of six or seven is fastened upside down to an aluminium frame and a technician is squeezing drops from a syringe into its nostrils.

When Fully Olbin holds out the next photograph Vail fails to respond. "You haven't seen them all. There's more."

"I've seen enough."

"This one shows what happens to the child in the frame when the drops have eaten into the brain tissue,—"

"I can imagine it, thank you." Vail is ashen to the lips and doesn't feel too well. "Is there a purpose behind all this?"

"Behind all what? The U.M.P.S. Programme?"

"No, you showing me these pictures," Vail says, handing back the ones he has looked at.

"Not so long ago you resolved to kill somebody and lacked the opportunity. Now you have the opportunity you've lost the resolve. We should like to rekindle it."

"Why did he murder my wife?" Vail says, pointing his finger at Urban Brown.

144

"He's got so used to killing he can't help himself. He's a sick man."

"And yet you expect me to help you, to do you some 'good'. How can you ask me to do anything at all for you when that man there killed my wife?" Vail says, weeping. "That man *sitting* there."

"What do you want me to do?" Fully Olbin asks gently. "Kill him for you in revenge?"

"I don't know, I don't know. But he *murdered* her and you bring me here and ask me to help *you*."

"Crazy things happen all the time today, on both sides of the wire. We're all of us crazy to some degree. It's not his fault; but I can have him killed if it will make you feel any better."

"Tell me why I should help you after what he did," Vail says, weeping.

"Well." Fully Olbin considers for a moment. "For one thing, our aims happen to coincide,—or they did coincide until you lost your resolve. For another, you will be revenging the murder of your daughter. And thirdly, though I hate to mention it, it seems so trivial under the circumstances, you still owe us a favour in exchange for the one Tex did you. Without the *Temporal* you probably wouldn't have made it past Watford Gap."

"I made that promise in better days," Vail says. "I had some hope then. I thought that if I could get to London I could save Bev," weeping less now, a tiny cold formation of rage in his stomach making his tears flow less.

"These aren't better days, I agree," Fully Olbin says in a gentle tone of voice. For a big black man he has a very gentle manner. "Of course I can't promise you that they will ever get better. I'm being completely honest with you. And I can't force you to kill somebody if you don't want to. But now, or very soon, you will have the Opportunity, and Angie said that given the motivation you wouldn't hesitate."

"Angie told you that about me?" Vail says in disbelief, having stopped weeping altogether.

"Yes."

145

"Angie,—the girl I live with,—told *you* that?"

"Correct."

"I don't understand,—why should she? When?"

"Jack," Fully Olbin smiles, "Angie lives with you because I asked her to. I told her to get to know you, which she did, and gain your confidence. It was much easier than we could have hoped for."

"Angie is Fully's girl," Tex Rivett chips in.

"Do you mean she belongs to this terrorist cell?" Vail says incredulously.

Fully Olbin smiles down at him. "That's how we were able to keep tabs on you and how we knew that Wayde Dake Ass. Inc. had followed up Tex's phone calls and compiled a report on the four of us. Fortunately he couldn't discover Angie's identity. You don't think you met her by chance at that party, do you?"

"Yes . . . I thought . . ."

Fully Olbin is shaking his head. "Nothing is ever that simple, Jack, not in this day and age. I thought you'd have learnt that by now."

"Christ, and I told her everything."

"Yes, it was a very full account." Fully Olbin doesn't have to reach up very far to take down one of the S-shaped meat hooks with sharpened ends hanging from the metal bars. "About your wife and child and the green van on the M6, and picking up Brown, and meeting Tex at Sandbach, and what happened in Spaghetti Junction and your experiences at Watford Gap, and then at the Newport Pagnell checkpoint and driving along the A422, the supermarket and the hospital, the milk tanker and all that stuff. It was a very full account indeed."

"So," Vail says, taking out his handkerchief and blowing his nose, "you've just been waiting. Would you have waited and waited . . . I mean just kept on waiting until I was where you wanted me to be? It could have taken years."

Fully Olbin throws the hook the full length of the meat locker with sufficient force for it to be embedded in the lead-lined wall.

"We nudged it along here and there. Angie planted the idea in Bryce Ransom's head that a programme along the lines of

146

Bootstraps might be just what the public wanted and in Virgie Hance's head that you might be just the person to front it. It was very simple. Childishly easy, in fact. And of course they leapt at it."

"You know," Vail says, "when you brought me here I thought you were going to kill me." He doesn't know whether to feel relieved or disappointed.

"That was the last thing on our minds,—we want *you* to kill for *us*."

"Then we'll be quits," Vail says. "That will be the favour I owe you, will it?"

"Paid in full," Fully Olbin confirms.

Vail thinks this over for a moment or two. "Are those photographs you showed me genuine?"

"From Govt files."

"The things in them are actually going on right this minute?"

"Everything Brown told you is true. Dumping toxic waste near to densely populated areas, discharging radioactive effluent into streams and rivers next to schools, reducing health care to the point where the system breaks down completely, conducting so-called medical/scientific experiments to control and inhibit the population. All true. That's what the U.M.P.S. Programme is all about."

"What does it stand for?"

"It's a Govt departmental euphemism: Unwashed Masses Prefer Suicide. It confirms their own belief in what is right and best, and is a sop to their conscience. They want to believe, and do believe, that people would rather die than lead empty brutish lives, and as only a very few can lead decent lives, this is the expedient solution. It makes it easier for everyone."

Fully Olbin delves into the photographs and holds one up for Vail to see: the workmen planting saplings in raw earth recently levelled by a bulldozer. "I thought you might have recognised the five high-rise buildings in the background. If you had there would be no need to convince you or say anything more."

After studying the photograph Vail is none the wiser.

147

"Zuttor Estate taken two years ago. You lived at Number 431, so my informant tells me."

[12]

The suavely diminutive and softly spoken Ed Flesh is on the phone to Vail, his voice like the distant rush of the sea inside a mouse's ear.

"Have you heard the good news? The programme's won an award."

"Really?" Vail says, sitting up in the oval bath. "The U.M.P.S. Programme, you mean?"

"No, no, not the U.M.P.S. Programme,—*Bootstraps*. Your show. They think it's wonderful. That piece on the Baths . . ."

"Who does?"

"Everyone. It's a smash. I'm raising your asking price by fifty per cent and putting in a statutory profits clause. In the meantime don't open any supermarkets or endorse anything without my say-so."

"I don't intend to open any supermarkets."

"Then don't. I think I've clinched a six-figure exclusive merchandising contract for TV commercials and a ten-week promo tour."

"Who with?"

"The Milk Marketing Board."

"Not milk," Vail says firmly. "Anything but milk."

"I've only sold your mouth and larynx. The rest of you is up for grabs."

"Not milk, Flesh, I'm sorry. Beer, Coke, piss, vomit, diarrhoea, you name it and I'll endorse it. But not milk."

Ed Flesh shrugs his sloping shoulders in his silk-mohair suit. "All right, Jack, have it your way. But if Selina had your attitude she'd still be fucking politicians for a living. And you know something, Jack? She hasn't had to fuck anyone she didn't want to in over *two years*. Think about it."

148

Vail watches Ed Flesh's blurred image through the rising steam,—funny how he looks small even on the screen.

"The last thing we want happening to you is what happened to The Pox, remember."

"Why, what happened to them?"

"They've gone bust. *Burn Down the Schools* grossed $26 million worldwide and instead of putting it into securities as I advised they went into audio equipment, electronic games, TV leasing, car hire, insurance and fast food franchising. I told them they'd get their fingers burned but would they listen to Flesh? Sunk every cent into four offshore companies for tax avoidance and then guaranteed equity capital of quarter-million apiece to a Swiss outfit specialising in share dealing, commodity trading, venture capital and split dividend futures. Lucky they've got their property interests, recording studios and stock portfolio to fall back on or they'd really be in trouble."

"I suppose they would," Vail says, soaping his chest thoughtfully.

"So don't let that happen to you, Jack."

"No, I won't."

"Take a leaf out of Josh's book. He never invests more than $100,000 at any one time. That's how his LA operation started,—nothing wild, nothing high-flown. Now look at him. Of course he prays a good deal."

"So I believe."

"The presentation's on the seventeenth."

"What presentation?"

"The award presentation, nationwide TV live, the PM in person. Has Wayde Dake Ass. Inc. been in touch?"

"No, why?"

"He's worried about you. His operative lost contact for over three hours. They thought you'd been kidnapped or killed."

"I'm still here. Must have been a malfunction."

"Well, take care. You're a very precious commodity, Jack. You're being watched every minute night and day, don't forget. We can't afford to lose you."

The cold hard formation of rage in Vail's stomach, his only

149

viable form of human emotion, has been joined by another of incipient gathering excitement. The two bubbles reside side by side like ovaries awaiting fertilisation. Soon they will swell and divide and multiply and take possession of the organism that is host to them. Vail's identity, precarious at the best of times, is soon to be taken over by a monster.

[13]

It was common knowledge that the Libyans had the Bomb and speculation now grew rife that they had made it available to the INLA. The pubs, restaurants, cafes and video porn shops were agog with rumour about when, where and how such a device might be deployed. Would the target be military or civilian? Would they have the nerve and the capability to try for London, the seat of power, or, say, somewhere unimportant like Reading or Bournemouth?

For a while these fearful conjectures were confined to the streets and not discussed openly in the media: everyone knew and yet the Govt embargo prohibited public dissemination of such material in case it caused panic and alarm.

The point was soon reached, however, when something official had to be said, and the PM made a special broadcast on the Jimmy Young programme, explicitly warning both the Libyans and the INLA that any aggressive act against the United Kingdom would be met with the sternest retaliatory measures. Grim-faced, the PM intoned: "We shall brook no quarter, nor shall the sword sleep in my hand. Anyone, and I do mean anyone, Jimmy,—I may call you Jimmy, mayn't I?—who dares to drop the Bomb on a single square centimetre of this green and pleasant land drops it on me and my kith and kin. This sceptred isle has repelled boarders since time immemorial and we shall repel them now, and yes, I say, keep on repelling them. Let me just say this: beware 'for whom the bell tolls, it might toll for thee.'"

Next day the papers carried red banner headlines.

150

PM SLAMS DAGOES AND MICKS . . . "DON'T TRY IT SUNSHINE—OR ELSE!" WARNS PM . . . PM "BROOKS NO QUARTER" AND TELLS LIBS "WATCH IT!" . . . UK COULD FLATTEN SAND DUNES "AT A STROKE"— OFFICIAL . . . DUNKIRK SPIRIT IN DOWNING STREET* ran one headline, which got the editor sacked and his background investigated by Special Branch.

Meanwhile, as might be expected, Vail is having problems of his own. Three or four times now he has returned home from work to find his chauffeur-cum-terrorist cell ringleader Fully Olbin humping Angie in his (Vail's) bed. Of course Fully Olbin has explained the nature of their relationship, which Vail, having no other choice, is prepared to accept; but what he finds difficult to come to terms with is Fully Olbin's and Angie's brash and blatant behaviour. Fair enough, she was Fully Olbin's girl, the black man had prior claim,—but this usurping of his rights in the broad light of day, without the least circumspection or consideration, Vail finds unsettling and even vaguely distasteful. He doesn't feel like climbing onto a warm woman still wet and panting from exertions he himself has witnessed on walking through the door. After a hard day at the studio it is a bit too much. He is not sure he is prepared to tolerate it.

Angie lies gently steaming in the hot trough of the bed while Fully Olbin pulls on his boots and zips up his flies and Vail stands by the door kicking his heels.

"Christ Jesus Almighty, you should have heard me moan," Angie says luxuriously. "Fully hammers away like my clit's made of steel and there's no tomorrow."

*Hastily amended in later editions to HARRODS' SPIRIT AT NO. 10.

151

"I'm very pleased to hear it," Vail replies, tight-lipped politeness masking tiredness and shortness of temper. Why is she telling *him* this? The last thing he wants to hear is that a black man is good,—and by implication better than him,—at it.

"Have a good day, darling?"

"Not bad. Aren't you supposed to be working?"

"There was a bomb alert in Marylebone High Street and we were let off early." Angie smiles impishly. "And when I got here Fully was cleaning the car . . ."

"You don't have to elaborate. Is this all part of your search for the meaning of life?" Vail asks sarcastically. "The never-ending orgasm? It seems to me,—"

"It seems to me you'd better shut your mouth," Fully Olbin says, rising to his immense height. "Who are you to criticise, anyway? Somebody who murdered his wife and child in cold blood. Button it."

Vail feels a flush of outrage on his cheeks.

"In case you've forgotten, it was your colleague, your fellow so-called terrorist, who killed my wife. The man's a raving psychopath. Don't dare accuse *me* of that despicable act."

"The cops don't know that, do they?" says Fully Olbin silkily.

Vail gapes. He's seen both the subservient black chauffeur and the authoritative terrorist ringleader sides to Fully Olbin, but not this snide, underhand, smirking blackmailer before. Life is full of nasty surprises.

"And don't forget what you've promised to do in return for the favour you owe us," Fully Olbin continues, rubbing it in and buttoning his tunic. "We're watching you every minute night and day. You'd better deliver."

Vail says coldly, "You don't have to remind me of my responsibilities. But don't you forget I'm doing it for my own personal reasons, not for some tinpot terrorist organisation that can't even blow up a nuclear power station properly. Pathetic."

Here in his own flat he feels strong and capable of righteous anger, surrounded by his own possessions, whereas not too long ago in the meat locker his bowels had creaked with fear. Strange

152

how you could feel strong one minute and weak the next, strong and then weak, strength and weakness alternating in the same frame, altering everything about you, even your physical appearance. When you were strong you could conquer the world and when you were weak you wanted to crawl into a hole in the skirting board and rot.

"Come on if you're coming." Angie is impatient. "I'm cooling off fast here. I can take another while I'm in the mood."

Vail stares at her with contempt for perhaps a moment or two, loosens his tie, unbuttons his shirt.

[14]

Vail crosses Knightsbridge, passes through the barbed-wire checkpoint at the Brompton Road intersection, submits to a body search after which he is allowed to enter the sandbagged portals of Harrods, its remaining display windows criss-crossed with brown tape. Inside he pauses to inspect a baby sealskin belt costing £128, decides not to buy, and moves on.

In a mirror he catches sight of himself in false beard and redundant spectacles, a disguise made necessary by his famous face. Without it he would be accosted every few paces by admirers wanting his autograph and others brimming over with envy and malice, intent on doing him physical harm. There were some around whose lives were so meaningless, insignificant and empty of purpose that they had an overwhelming urge to change the course of history, no matter how fractionally, and the quickest way was to kill a media personality. Thus a loser and no-hoper, a *swmbwl*, could make the headlines for just one day and have the satisfaction of knowing that his act had altered the mental landscape of millions: the cipher of his life would have been granted momentary relevance and validity.

As an instance of this, a few days ago Vail had been followed by a young man with large red boots and plaited hair who had spotted Vail in a tube station and stuck to him at a distance of fifteen metres for half an hour or more. Down the escalator they went together, along semi-circular tiled tunnels, down several twisting flights of steps, and onto the platform where Vail pretended to study a map of the underground while his pursuer fiddled ineffectually with the worn silver knobs of a vending machine. When the train arrived Vail stepped inside and the youth did likewise through a door farther along the carriage. During the short journey the young man stared fixedly at Vail through the undergrowth of newspapers, umbrellas and briefcases and made no pretence of the fact that he was waiting to see which station Vail got out at.

Sure enough, as Vail exited, so did the youth, and now the process was reversed,—up several flights of twisting steps, along semi-circular tiled tunnels, up the escalator, the same fifteen-metre distance rigorously maintained between them. At the top of the escalator Vail turned sharp right and right again, and instead of taking one of the two tunnels marked Bakerloo and Central sidled round in a complete circle and slid back nimbly onto the down escalator once again.

As the muscles released their stranglehold on his intestines (it isn't pleasant being followed, even in a crowded public place) he glanced with a relieved perspiring grin over his shoulder only to find the young man in the red boots and plaited hair fifteen metres behind, staring at him without expression.

Shaking off his would-be assassin hadn't been easy; it had been a lucky fluke that at Covent Garden Vail had been the third from last person into the elevator and that when the gates clashed shut the youth was trapped about halfway along the tiled corridor with the next consignment.

The sweat drying rapidly on his face in the cool night air, his chest and back slippery under his clothing, Vail was waiting at the pedestrian crossing outside the station when another youth, this time black, had jostled his shoulder and mumbled something about finding the way to Chelsea. Vail shook his head dumbly and dodged out through the traffic, his knees trembling with fear. In the pub he drank a double whisky straight down to calm his nerves and then immediately had to go to the lavatory to shed his load of molten diarrhoea. The lavatory was of the old-fashioned Victorian type, with high ornate ceiling and tiled cubicles and solid walnut doors that could have withstood a battering-ram. It was a haven of peace and calm, sitting there, the air circulating round his steaming flanks, and he could have sat forever had it not been for the bass gurgling moan that came from the cubicle to his left. Hurriedly wiping himself and buttoning up, Vail got out fast, merely swilling his hands under the tap and wafting them as he walked to dry them. The experience had shaken him and he wasn't anxious to repeat it, hence the beard and glasses.

On the third floor he meanders through soft furnishings and is bent double examining a carpet for the Kite mark when a thin face with a beaked nose separating watery brown eyes is thrust into his.

"How goes it, old sport? Still making a fortune at Thames, I see. Fancy meeting you here!"

"You're not supposed to recognise me."

Pete Rarity frowns. "Why not?" Then his face clears. "Oh, you mean the beard and specs? Spot you a mile off, John, with 'em or without 'em. What are you frightened of, being followed in the underground again?"

Vail straightens up and gazes at him narrowly. "How do you know about that? Have you been following me?"

"It was all over the papers, John. Centre-spread in the *Sun*, beard, glasses, the lot. Wearing that get-up is like carrying a placard with your name on it. They even had an interview with the guy following you, what was his name,—?"

"You mean it was all set up?" He is sweating under the beard and there are bits of hair stuck to his lips.

"Wouldn't put it past them; everything is nowadays. You know what the tabloids are like, anything for a giggle."

Vail has heard of the conspiracy theory of history but can he really accept this as true? Why, it would mean that every person is suspect, that no actions are innocent. Even Pete Rarity being here,

155

in this light, could be interpreted as due to ulterior motives, for nefarious purposes, instead of mere happenstance.

Together they crunch through broken glass into white goods and look at the freezers, roomy enough to take an ox. Vail tries not to think of the meat locker, and, by association, Fully Olbin: for all he knows the bug in his balls might be attuned to picking up his thought-waves as well.

"I hear there's to be a presentation," Pete Rarity smiles. "By no less a person than the PM. You *have* come up in the world since that lukewarm cup of coffee in the Soho porn theatre."

"What presentation?"

"Of the award, old man. Your TV show. 'Best Current Affairs Entertainment Programme.' You've been told, haven't you? I thought Ed Flesh,—"

"Yes, I've been told," Vail says shortly.

"It's very well thought of in Govt circles. They like its attitude, its philosophy. Make the spassies sweat for their leg-irons and wheelchairs instead of getting them on a silver platter. There are no free lunches any more, not in this day and age."

Vail is distracted by something and can't think what. Something is niggling at him.

Pete Rarity goes on, "You swim by your own efforts or sink in your own waste products. *Homo sapiens* crawled out of the primordial slime and that is the true human condition. Anyone who thinks otherwise is living in a fool's paradise and is in for a rude awakening."

What the hell is it?

"I have to be going," Vail announces abruptly. "There's a technical run-through at three o'clock."

"What about a freezer? Aren't you going to buy one?"

"No, I was just browsing. Freezers don't interest me."

"If you're going I may as well come with you."

They pass the mounds of blackened debris and enter the lift and glide downwards in silence except for the subdued whine of hydraulics. The operator is a big strapping fellow in a dark blue uniform with triangular shoulder flashes picked out in silver thread. The lift continues past the ground floor and descends to the basement. The doors open on a cavernous concrete emptiness stretching dimly away. Vail hesitates.

"This isn't the way I came in."

"Alternative exit, sir. Security precautions for our better-known customers."

"Which way?"

"To your left. Follow the green arrows."

Vail steps out followed by Pete Rarity in his shabby suit and broken shoes. The green arrows on the walls are very faint, barely discernible. Easy to mistake your way, take a wrong turning, and find yourself lost. Where does this come out, Vail wonders, if they're below street level? Harrods' consideration for its clientele has certainly taken a turn for the worse.

After a while he realises that there are two sets of footsteps behind him, Pete Rarity's and the lift operator's. He is about to say something,—suggest the lift operator lead the way as presumably, being an employee. he is familiar with the layout of the place,—when the man says:

"Nearly there. Through the door to your left."

It is warm down here in the basement, close to the boiler room, the air dense and humid, and Vail feels itchy and uncomfortable under the beard. He goes through the door into a long passage no more than three feet wide, lined with silver-clad pipes, and at once the heat is suffocating.

He gasps. "Are you sure we can get out this way?"

"This'll do," says Pete Rarity to the lift operator, who touches his cap and stands four-square in the doorway. "Stop here."

Vail turns round. "Are you talking to me?"

"This doesn't lead anywhere so there's no point in going on." Pete Rarity's hand dips inside his threadbare jacket and pulls out a small plastic card which he holds up for Vail to see in the dingy light: a serial number, some fine print which Vail can't read, and in large black capitals the letters UCP.

"Heard of us?" Pete Rarity asks, raising his eyebrows so that

157

vee-shaped wrinkles ruffle his narrow unattractive forehead.

Vail has. "Though I must say I'm surprised. I always thought they were a northern delicacy and hadn't caught on down south."

"What hadn't?"

"Tripe, pigs' trotters, cow heel and black puddings."

"Tripe,—?" Pete Rarity says. "Not with you, John."

"You're a rep for United Cattle Products, am I right? I hadn't realised they were so popular down here."

"Look. Under-Cover Police. Nothing to do with tripe or that other stuff you mentioned."

"Oh, sorry," Vail says. It was a genuine mistake. Does this mean that Pete Rarity is more important than he has hitherto assumed? He tries to recall if in the past he has been actually openly nasty to Pete Rarity and doesn't think he has: just as well, because in this day and age people bear grudges, sometimes for years, just waiting for the opportunity to get their own back, stick the knife in, twist it.

"I'd like to ask you one or two questions."

"Great. Sure. Go ahead." Vail shrugs. "Why not?"

Pete Rarity smiles. "Why don't you take the beard off, you look hot."

"I am a bit," Vail says. He takes most of it off, leaving straggly wisps on his chin and upper lip. "Phew, that's better. Anyway, I don't suppose anyone will recognise me down here will they?"

"Only me and Special Constable MUTCH," Pete Rarity says, which makes Vail realise where he's seen the lift operator before. Until now he hasn't looked at him properly, which is the usual thing with lift operators. "We,—I'm speaking now for the UCP,—have been keeping a friendly eye on you, John. You've attained a position of considerable power and influence in the media and we don't want to see you getting embroiled with the wrong sort of people. You know who I mean."

"Television producers?"

"Not television producers. They're fine, politically and morally okay, providing they're kept in their place. We're referring to undesirable elements in society at large who may be tempted to

158

use you for their own purposes. I'm sure you know the types I mean." He arches one eyebrow.

"Not really," Vail says, playing dumb.

"No one's contacted you then and asked you to do them a small 'favour'?"

Vail gives a wide-eyed shake of the head.

"You see," Pete Rarity goes on thoughtfully, "we are naturally somewhat concerned about those missing hours when your bug stopped transmitting and we lost you on the screen. Any idea what happened?"

"As far as I can recall I was at home in bed fast asleep."

"Were you screwing?"

Vail pretends to try to remember, then pretends to give it up as a bad job. "I can't honestly say. Could have been. I screw most nights but that particular night I might not have been. You think if I had been it might have affected the bug, sent it haywire?"

"Shouldn't have, it's the latest model. Who might you have been screwing, do you think?"

Vail mops his brow. Why Harrods consider it necessary to maintain their basement at this unholy temperature he can't imagine. "Various people. I don't keep track. Being a famous media personality I have ample scope and opportunity. How long have you been with the UCP?"

"Seven years."

Vail shows surprise. "And all along I thought you were a down-and-out fringer like me. You kept up the pretence well," he says flatteringly. "And still do."

"Part and parcel of the training. If I hadn't been a member of the UCP you'd never have got the job. I dropped a word here and there in the right quarter. Don't you remember who it was rang you up to tell you of Bryce Ransom's interest and who introduced you to him in the first place?" Pete Rarity wears a fat smug smile.

Vail is properly nonplussed.

"We set you up with Angie, of course," Pete Rarity says, compounding Vail's frozen incredulity.

"You mean she works for *you*?"

"On a part-time basis. We spotted you as a likely candidate right from the start but it would have been foolhardy to put all that your way without keeping a close watch on you. Angie updates us on your social contacts and political affiliations and so on."

"You mean she spies on me?"

"Not spies exactly, that's putting it too strong. She reports all your movements, who you see, and tells us what you say and think. More a kind of friendly surveillance."

"And I thought when I met her at Bryce Ransom's party that she fancied me."

Pete Rarity casts a sidelong smirk at SC MUTCH standing stolidly in the doorway, dripping. "Hardly, John. You stank. I had one hell of a job persuading her to take you home." He sniggers,—"You really thought she was attracted to you?",—and shakes his head pityingly.

It is something of a struggle for Vail to come to terms with this newly revealed aspect of a situation he thought he had assimilated and thoroughly understood,—rather like learning your name isn't your name and you're not the person you thought yourself to be. It opens up chasms of doubt. All along he had seen himself as the victim of arbitrary circumstances, whereas it now appeared that the entire affair had been rigged, stage-managed, from the start. This posed the question, did he prefer the chaotic sway of random forces,—God playing dice,—or these devious backstage machinations as arbiters and directors of his fate? Both were equally chilling. One proposed (a proposition he had accepted unthinkingly) that events were acausal and had little or no relationship one with another, that the world functioned by a series of happy coincidences; while the other had it that we are all locked into an iron grid dictatorship, a totalitarian state of circumstance which directs our moves with cold clinical passion . . .

Either way Vail is unhappy, and made uneasier still by the sudden switch from one to the other: he was content to stand on shifting sand and is disturbed to find bedrock underneath his feet. Is this why Pete Rarity brought him down to Harrods' basement, to impress upon him that the surface world has architectural as well as metaphysical foundations?

Symbolism, for God's sake?

"You're probably wondering why I brought you down here? Yes? Do I see you nod? I thought so. I'm a pretty astute judge of character. The reason is, John, that we've received a report from beyond the wire that the bodies of your wife and child have been discovered in shallow graves. One had been strangled, the other smothered in a tartan blanket, within two to three days of each other according to forensic evidence. SC MUTCH and his colleague SC HUCK have testified that both these persons were alive and well when they inspected your vehicle on the M6. Have you anything to say?"

"My daughter wasn't at all well, she was suffering from some disease or other, toxic waste poisoning or radiation sickness."

"Even so, she didn't die of natural causes, and neither did your wife. Have you anything to say on this matter? Can you offer an explanation, convincing or otherwise?"

Vail moves as far away as possible from the blisteringly hot pipes in their silvery cladding, though due to the narrowness of the passage this isn't very far. All three of them are perspiring heavily. Droplets are gathering under SC MUTCH's chin.

"My superiors have instructed me not to return without an answer of some sort," Pete Rarity warns. "Murder outside the wire isn't an indictable offence, but nevertheless records have to be completed, files collated and kept up to date. In any case you wouldn't be charged, being who you are."

"It wouldn't be held against me if I said I'd murdered them?"

"Not if you had good reason and didn't step out of line. After all, two less mouths to feed. You would be tried and executed only if it was felt to be in the public interest."

Vail is curious to know how he could be executed. "We abolished the death penalty years ago."

Pete Rarity gives a little smile. "On paper yes. It makes us look libertarian and progressive. But there's more than one way to skin a cat."

"You mean to say people are actually killed outside the law?" Vail asks naively. "By the state?"

"To all intents and purposes their useful lives are terminated," Pete Rarity concedes. "It's all perfectly humane and needn't concern you."

"On whose orders?"

Pete Rarity's smile hardens into a mask. "I must repeat: it's none of your business. What needs to be done is done. Trust Forte."

"I had nothing to do with those murders," Vail says.

"You must have had *something* to do with them, John," Pete Rarity insists gently. "It was your wife and your child and they were last seen in your company. Who else could it have been?"

"It wasn't me, couldn't have been, I was on this side of the wire. I'd gone for help."

"You didn't come through the wire until after they were dead. The forensic evidence and the record of your entry together confirm that. Why not tell us the truth? It's a mere detail, nothing more. It would be far better off your conscience, and you wouldn't be required to pay for it unless, as I say, you did something that displeased us such as fraternising with undesirable elements in society at large, television producers aside. Get it off your chest, you'll feel cleansed."

"I didn't do it."

Pete Rarity looks sad. A sigh escapes his lips. He grips Vail's genitalia through his clothing, though not hard enough to hurt.

"I could order SC MUTCH to press you against these steam pipes and hold you there till they swell up into a blister too big to put back inside your trousers. But really I'm averse to that. And yet there again I have to submit a satisfactory report to my superiors. So I find myself facing something of a dilemma."

When Vail doesn't reply he unzips his trousers and delves soft

162

fingers inside and exposes Vail to the humid air. Vail is yielding and pulpy in his warm hand, sluglike.

"What's it to be, ladies' pride and joy or second degree burns and permanent scar tissue?"

Vail doesn't entertain the slightest doubt that SC MUTCH will carry out the order. There will be a struggle, a few grunts, an ineffectual scuffle on the concrete floor, but in the end Vail knows he will succumb.

His tongue rasps like leather in his parched mouth. He says:

"I killed Bev, my daughter."

"You've saved your cock," Pete Rarity says, separating the member in question and pushing it aside. "Now what about your cookies?"

"I killed Mira, my wife."

"How did you do it?" Pete Rarity asks, still holding him.

"Strangled one, smothered the other, buried them both."

"That's splendid," Pete Rarity says, releasing him. "All your problems are over. Well done."

"What happens now?"

"Nothing. You make yourself decent and go to your technical run-through with a clear conscience, secure in the knowledge that we're watching you every minute day and night."

[15]

With the exception of the terrorists everyone was at the presentation ceremony held in the PM's bunker underneath Horse Guards Parade on the second Saturday in December. This venue was made necessary by the sudden sharp escalation of recent events involving the INLA-Libyan Popular Front and their threat, taken seriously by the authorities, to detonate a nuclear device within the environs of London.

Fully Olbin, as he confided to Vail, was none too pleased. "They're just trying to grab the limelight and make themselves a

163

household name like Bovril. Underground terrorist cells all over the country are furious."

"I would have thought they'd have been pleased to see the seat of power blown to smithereens," Vail said, puzzled. "Isn't that the object of the exercise?"

"There was no joint consultative meeting," Fully Olbin explained sulkily. "And anyway, they simply want to rupture the fabric of society whereas we want to replace it with a Neo-Trotskyist fabric. It's nothing but downright selfish."

"Have they really got the Bomb or are they bluffing?"

"They've got it all right. The question is, can they deliver it?"

"Can they?"

"With a combination of Arabs and Micks, what do you think?"

After passing through the metal detector arch, which gave Vail a nasty twitch in the scrotum, he and Angie are given a brisk and expert frisking by the guards on the door before being finally allowed to enter. The hall reminds him of the interior of a large silage barn, ceiling and walls one continuous sloping piece supported by curved metal girders reaching to the floor. The floor is concrete, which makes the scuffling of feet sound hollow, like in a railway station.

However, being eighty feet below ground makes everyone feel reasonably safe and quite jolly.

As is usual at such gatherings, cliques have already formed. Vail's clique is at the bar: Laine Vere Jumper, Mrs Stretcher, Bryce Ransom, Virgie Hance, Suze, the director, with Ed Flesh and Wayde Dake making up the party. Tonight, Vail is the star attraction. Passers-by smile at him familiarly, even though he doesn't know them from Adam, and important people like Ministers and Under-Secretaries nod and smirk in his direction so that he feels naked and exposed to the elements. Such is the price of media fame.

After a couple of drinks Vail begins to loosen up. He had

164

debated with himself whether or not to take a *Temporal* capsule, to get him through the evening, and had decided, he's now glad to say, not to. He might even begin to enjoy himself later.

Wire-frame spectacles winking, thin neck writhing with blue veins above his ruffled shirt and velvet bow tie, Bryce Ransom makes a little speech. Vail listens dumbly to the spill of words, nodding when the others nod, smiling when they do, throwing back his head and laughing along with the rest. It is only when the speech is over and the others look towards him expectantly that Vail realises he was the object of Bryce Ransom's gibberish and is expected to respond. What had been said about him? Was it a eulogy? Had he been praised, congratulated? Was he being thanked for his part in making *Bootstraps* such a resounding success?

Vail shrugs modestly and stares at his shuffling feet. "Well. I don't know what to say. What can I say? All I *can* say is that it was a team effort and that we all deserve, collectively, whatever's coming to us. That's all I have to say."

Virgie Hance squints at him greedily and slips him a slow lingering lascivious wink through the wraith of cigarette smoke curling up from the corner of her mouth.

". . . . . A noble sentiment succinctly expressed," drawls Laine Vere Jumper in his out-of-sync fashion. He is exquisitely attired in a brocade tuxedo with midnight blue velvet lapels and trousers with a shiny stripe down the sides.

"Unilever and Rowntree Mackintosh are going to go bananas for endorsement rights after this," chortles the neatly diminutive Ed Flesh, a happy smile wrapped round a fat cigar. "Hell, Jack, the lobes of your ears alone could be worth ten grand apiece! Watch out Steve Davis, stand aside Jimmy Saville, make way Bob Monkhouse!"

Everyone laughs delightedly, even Laine Vere Jumper, who has never heard of these people; his tastes run to Mozart, Proust and Cardinal Newman, though he did once see a television programme, many moons ago.

All along Vail has been wondering when the PM will put in an appearance. The award is to be presented personally, he has been told, an Opportunity he has looked forward to ever since he stood on the pavement outside the electrical retailer's these many weeks past. The events beyond the wire are now a murky racial memory residing in the base of his brain, though the desire they gave rise to remains.

As for Angie, he is undecided; will she encourage him in the act, indeed insist that he carry it out, or balk his attempt and report him to the UCP? Where, if anywhere, does she stand?

There is an explosion of flashlights and everyone turns to see what the commotion is all about. At first Vail thinks it is the PM, but it is in fact Selina Southorn making her entrance in a sequinned flesh coloured body stocking artfully torn in the most alluring places. Literally taken aback, Vail steps on the toe of Laine Vere Jumper, who utters a debonair oath. The reason for Vail's reaction is that hitherto he has only seen Selina Southorn in video pornlets and TV commercials and has assumed, not unnaturally, that she is a full-grown woman. But this creature, standing nipples akimbo in an admiring circle, is no more than four feet high! Beautifully proportioned it is true, but a midget nonetheless. No wonder the studs who serviced her on screen appeared as prime specimens of hulking manhood with dongs like bazookas,—any ordinary man would seem stupendously equipped alongside this child-woman, the height if not the build of a nine-year-old.

Soon she is lost to view in a scrum of Cabinet Ministers and the hall resumes its conversational buzz; the air of anticipation is growing.

The highlight of the evening is to be a "choir" made up of showbiz celebrities and media personalities who are to sing a specially-composed song in the PM's honour. To assemble such an array of

166

talent on a commercial stage would cost millions, yet here they all are, offering their services free, gratis and for nothing.

There is much friendly badinage, joshing and backslapping as they line up, and these genial, benevolent spirits infect the rest of the gathering like nerve gas. It's a wonderful life down here in the bunker.

Angie gasps and nudges Vail excitedly, thrilled to the core at having recognised Jimmy Saville, Bob Monkhouse, Kenny Everett, Jimmy Tarbuck, Sharon Davis, Vince Hill, Lyndsey de Paul, Steve Davis and Anthony Quayle, amongst many others. A collective halo or aura seems to surround these exalted personages, as if drab mundanity had been banished, if only temporarily, and replaced by real vibrant life. The dusty shadows in which most people live out their lives are dispelled and for a brief dizzy moment everyone basks in the penumbra of sensational immediacy blazing from the stage like radioactivity: "We are living in the actual here and now," they tell themselves, "an instant of momentous history in which it is better to be here than anywhere else",—a rare condition for human beings to find themselves in.

The PM has arrived, serenaded by the celebrity choir backed by The Pox. The tension and excitement are pretty well unbearable, not only because the PM is here in the flesh but also because rumour has swept the bunker that the INLA, aided and abetted by the Libyans, are all set to detonate the Bomb in central London. After all these weeks of waiting it is almost a relief.

A liveried flunkey touches Vail's arm and inquires in a sibilant whisper if he would care for another drink. The face between the lace cravat and the powdered wig is none other than that of the boy or youth, otherwise known as Tex Rivett.

"You must be crazy," Vail says through clenched jaws. "The place is crawling with security, not to mention *gwiches*."

"Keeping a friendly eye on you, sport."

"Don't you trust me?"

"Don't trust nobody, sunshine. Just don't forget we're here." He sidles away with a crooked leer and Vail beckons him back. "What?"

"Is Angie working for us or them?"

"What makes you ask?"

"I've been told she's really on their side. Could be a UCP plant."

"Relax," Tex Rivett grins greenly. "We know all about that; she's a double agent, working for us while pretending to work for them."

"So the UCP don't know what we're up to?"

"How could they? Unless somebody's told them."

Vail struggles to remember if he told them anything during the interrogation in Harrods' basement; but if he did the memory evades him. He feels scared. Is he losing his mind?

The party really is in full swing. It transpires that Selina Southorn is a frenetic sensation-seeking psychotic, taking the centre of the floor and twisting and gyrating her lovely tiny body to the sound of The Pox. She dances in a world of her own making, oblivious to the crowd and yet at the same time (Vail observes) occasionally catching the eye of the lead guitarist whose expressionless eyes never leave her cavorting figure in the criss-cross of spotlights.

Why does she dance alone? Vail wonders. Is it simply for the sake of exhibitionism? Her feet attack the floor, her eyes bore into nothingness, her body sways and dips and grinds with erotic abandon. For this child-woman the music is nothing more than an excuse for a public display of orgasmic fury.

Then it occurs to Vail that perhaps she is seeking her revenge. Like him she has a score to settle,—but against whom?

Knowing everyone of any importance, Laine Vere Jumper

introduces Vail to several Cabinet Ministers and Under-Secretaries. They comment enthusiastically on *Bootstraps* and praise his convincing portrayal of someone who has wrenched himself free from the common herd and made good solely by his own efforts. "A smashing example," murmurs one, and "Jolly fine show," smiles another.

"In my opinion you deserve nothing less than a bloody Oscar," the Minister for Deformed Imbeciles tells him fervently. "Tell me, have you always been an actor?"

Vail glances uncertainly at Laine Vere Jumper. "Not always. Only very recently."

"Even more commendable. You're damn' convincing, I will say that."

The talk moves on to other things: the success the Americans have had with the development of AIDS, which has drastically reduced the male homosexual population; and on this side of the Atlantic the importing of heroin from Pakistan to keep the kids docile, and in particular the U.M.P.S. Programme.

The Minister for Environmental Pollution waves aside the effusive compliments with a fleshy manicured hand. "It was nothing, nothing," he insists deprecatingly. "A simple equation. On the one side, several thousand tonnes of toxic and radioactive waste to be disposed of; on the other, large urban populations that had outlived their usefulness and quite frankly were a pain in the arse. Bring the two together and,—hey presto! Both problems solved at a stroke."

"Damn' brilliant, Henry; a masterstroke."

"Nice of you to say so, Cecil. I do think it worked rather well myself."

"No chance of the beastly stuff spreading down here, I suppose?" someone inquires with a twinge of unease.

The Minister smiles and shakes his head. "Trust Forte."

"Only there are rumours floating about that a number of Illegal Aliens have broached the wire. Don't like the sound of that."

"You mean breached the wire, surely?"

"Broached or breached, is it true?"

"Perhaps the odd one. But I shouldn't worry about it."

"I do worry about it, Henry. I don't view the prospect of getting a dose of dioxin poisoning with sanguinity. Does the PM know about it?"

"The PM never misses a trick, you know that." The Minister downs his drink with a flourish. "Let's stop all this morbid speculation. We're here to enjoy ourselves,—but I say, that Selina's a bit of a sexy tart, isn't she though?"

For a while Vail watches Selina Southorn in her frenetic lonely dance, overlooked by the louring dead gaze of the lead guitarist. Something will happen there before the night's out, given half a chance.

He goes to the toilet, relieves himself at the galvanised trough (as with everything else in the place, he is reminded of a farm) and washes his hands and face. There is perfume on the air; sandalwood. The harsh strip lighting makes him appear gaunt and skull-like with sunken eyes. Not at all like Jack Nicholson.

The washroom attendant deferentially proffers a soft snowy-white towel and as Vail sinks his face into it mutters, "So far so good, Jack. Keep it up."

"What are you doing here?"

"Just keeping a friendly eye on you," Pete Rarity says, hands clasped servilely in front of the gleaming lapels of his crisp white jacket. "Said I would. Don't disappoint us, will you?"

"I shouldn't like to disappoint anyone, least of all the UCP." Vail hands the towel back and walks to the door, where he pauses. Something is troubling him. "You did say that Angie works for you? I mean, she doesn't work for anyone else as far as you know?"

"They think she does," says Pete Rarity, ritually going through the motions of a washroom attendant, folding the used towel and dropping it into a plastic bin with a swing lid.

"'They' think she does?"

"An underground terrorist cell."

170

"So you know about that?"

"We're not fools, John." He takes a fresh towel from the pile and drapes it over his forearm and arranges the edges neatly. "They know she works for us but are under the impression that she really works for them when all the time she really works for us."

"She couldn't really *really* be working for them could she?"

"You mean working for them but working for us but working for them but working for us but really working for them?"

Vail nods.

"If she was we'd know about it."

"Not if they knew you knew about it."

"But then we'd know they knew we knew about it."

Vail is prepared to concede this; besides, the conversation is making his head spin. He tips Pete Rarity and returns to the barn-like hall whose curved walls and ceiling, streaming with condensation and nicotine, reverberate to the thumping beat of The Pox. Better not have anything else to drink. There are things to be done and he'll need all his wits about him.

What time is the presentation ceremony?

"What time is the presentation ceremony?"

"You're sweating. Are you nervous?" Angie says.

"No. Impatient. Why don't they just get on with it?"

Angie dimples in a smile. "Your turn will come. The preliminaries are as important as the event itself don't forget."

"Fuck the preliminaries."

"You've never been this nervous before."

"I am not nervous."

Angie doesn't look convinced. She says:

"You just have to be careful what you do, that's all."

What does she mean? "What does that mean?"

Is she tacitly giving him her approval or sounding a warning? *Whose bloody side is she on?*

"I've been told to say that and no more. The rest is up to you."

171

"That's all very well but where does it leave me?"

"I can't make the decision for you," Angie rebukes him.

"What is this, some heavy moral message or other? Every person responsible for his own destiny? Is this the answer to the famous meaning-of-life riddle you've been torturing yourself with?"

"That crap," Angie says, amused, shaking her head. "You really were taken in by it, weren't you? Just as you've been taken in by everything else. You're pretty dumb, Jack Vail."

Vail searches for a smart reply but can't think of one. He feels crushed and small. Perhaps the meaning of life boils down to this: you can never think of a smart reply when you need one.

[16]

Someone,—a Cabinet Minister most likely, or a Lord,—had planned it with the utmost meticulousness. As later reported, the DIs were led and carried and dragged in to a steady clapping chant and a uniform stamping of feet on the concrete floor. There were even a few cheers.

Stewards and security men arranged them like sacks of flour in a semi-circle round the dais on which the PM was to speak, in front of the throng so that the TV cameras had a clear, uninterrupted view. By this time the smell in the bunker was becoming quite foul, and together with the suppurating sores and rotting bodies of the dioxin victims caused several of the bystanders to faint clean away.

The VIPs and officials on the platform, however, all wore brave smiles, though one or two did take the occasional whiff from scented handkerchiefs concealed in their cuffs.

Not so the PM of course, whose beatific smile sprayed these unfortunate wretches with tolerance, understanding and forgiveness, duly caught and captured by the lenses and preserved on tape for the archives.

As was the limbless trunk of the little red-haired girl with

172

pigtails which squirmed up the steps and flopped onto the dais and rolled to a stop at the feet of the PM holding a bouquet of Freesias in its teeth. Tremors of emotion permeated the hall; tears leaked unashamedly and trickled down cheeks; the sorrowing heartfelt pity was palpable.

Graciously stooping to take the bouquet from the jaw of the child, the PM patted the pigtailed head and then, very gently, pushed the trunk with a polished toe so that it rolled off the platform and bumped down the steps where it was retrieved by a steward and set upright back in line. This incident was subsequently to be made famous by the media-managers who dubbed it "PM's Helping Toe for Heartbreak Imbecile".

Then came the PM's speech. A stirring performance that was to remain engravened on the hearts of all those present on that memorable and historic occasion. It began:

"Suffer little children to come unto me,"—provoking such a storm of applause even before the final syllable had rung out that it was several minutes before the PM was able to continue.

"Never let it be said," the speech resumed, "that we cannot find it in our hearts to be generous to those unfortunate imbeciles and mental defectives who, through no fault of their own, find themselves at the bottom of the heap of life. How can they be blamed for parental sloth, stupidity and ineptitude? Fathers too lazy to give a decent day's work for a decent day's pay. Mothers who smoke, watch television in the afternoons and patronise bingo establishments when they ought to be making the tea. Older brothers and sisters who get pregnant and stab old ladies in the eye, or vice versa, instead of caring and sharing and setting an example for their armless, legless and brainless siblings.

"These, the older ones, who ought to know better,—and I will not mince my words,—are the scum of the earth. Personally I've neither time or patience for them, and I fail to see how any decent, God-fearing, hard-working person can have time or patience for them either. You might say they're beyond hope, to which I would reply, 'Yes, I agree,—and the best place for people beyond hope is beyond the wire!'"

173

The PM sipped a glass of mineral water while the applause gathered itself and rose in a huge wave from the body of the hall and cascaded over the platform, drenching everyone in approving honeydew smiles.

The PM, however, remained stiff-necked and stern.

"Let us not forget also, that in some places which it would be invidious to mention, such as the Union of Soviet Socialist Republics and certain countries in Eastern Europe, Latin America and North Africa, peopled by mixed parentage races of a dusky hue, such unfortunates as these displayed before us tonight would not be acknowledged even to exist. Official secrets acts and juggling with Govt statistics would successfully disbar us from ever knowing about them in the first place. But in a democracy this can never happen. We *know* and we *care*.

"This alone makes our democratic freedoms all the more worth fighting for. What price democracy if we have to knuckle under and kow-tow to subversive terrorist groups and shiftless gangs of workshy layabouts and foreigners whose sole purpose is to impose their own brand of totalitarian ideology on the freedom-loving peoples of these islands? On this sceptred isle set in an azure sea? I for one will resist such encroachments with every breath in my body. I say this to them: Drop the Bomb, see if I care. When the dust has cleared you will find me still standing there in the rubble, bloody but unbowed, chin held high, fists raised in defiance. You may wipe us out but you will never defeat us. We are made of sterner stuff. We will fight, and continue to fight, in what is left of the streets, in the ruins of the supermarkets, in the debris of the video shops and software centres. We will never give in."

The deformed imbeciles round the dais were growing restless. Some were lying in the product of their own incontinence, dabbling in it with their stubby feelers. Movement for most of them was difficult, so they could only flop and squirm about in the spreading watery brown pool seeping from the elasticated sides of their plastic drawers. The more able and lively amongst them threw feeble handfuls of solid matter at one another, gurgling and mewling with glee, as malformed cretins are wont to do.

174

The crowd retreated to a respectable distance as the stench began to rise in dense torpid swathes.

Apparently oblivious to this, the PM went blithely on:

"I have heard it said that in these days of economic stringency we cannot afford moral standards. Nonsense. Hand in hand with sensible fiscal housekeeping must go the sternest and most rigorous moral strictures, set by those of us who know better as an example and guiding principle for the weak, the gullible, and the foolish. I put it to you: how can they live their lives usefully and fruitfully, and be of benefit to society, unless we have taken care to give them a framework of sound moral values within which to operate?

"Your glue-sniffer of today is your welfare state sponger of tomorrow. Wife-swapping may seem a harmless pastime to the uninitiated but it leads to moral degeneracy and a breakdown in family life. The child who doesn't attend Sunday school may well turn out to be another Yorkshire Ripper, or failing that a backstreet mugger who will stab a seventy-three year old lady in the eye for the few pence in her purse or rape and ravish a young innocent schoolgirl. Children who watch and revel in video nasties are income tax dodgers in the making.

"These are but a few examples I could cite of the danger areas,—and where our duty, as guardians of the nation's moral health, lies. It isn't enough to teach them geography and the three Rs. We must also teach them to respect other people's property. We must instil in them a suitable deference to their elders and betters. We must impress upon them that it is preferable to be seen rather than heard. Above all we must inculcate in the young those sterling qualities of politeness, docility, acquiescence, and not least of all to refrain from asking those silly questions which waste everyone's time and cause unnecessary fuss.

"It's all very well asking questions, I'm forever asking them; but there is a proper time and place for asking questions, and a correct manner, which older people recognise and accept and are perfectly happy to go along with. The young should learn from them.

"Of course an inquiring mind is all to the good, and I would be

175

the last person to discourage it. But at the risk of repeating myself I would just say this: people with inquiring minds very often find out things they would rather they hadn't learnt, and would be far better off remaining in ignorance of. A little knowledge can be a dangerous thing, as the poet says. Much more sensible to leave decisions to experts, those of us who have studied the various social, economic and moral problems in depth and have arrived at a balanced and informed opinion in the best interests of all our people."

Blue-uniformed stewards with mops and buckets were now swabbing the lumpy brown mess in which the imbeciles were squatting and squirming. Sandbags had been brought in and placed at strategic points in an attempt to contain its creeping spread;—indeed, unbeknown to the guests, their neat footwear had been spoiled by the lapping tide of bodily product, so intent were they on listening to the PM's speech and drinking in every word. Several found themselves stuck to the floor and had to be levered free.

"Which brings me to the highlight of the evening, the reason we're all down here in the first place, surrounded by these adorable little deformed bodies and grotesque faces, and that is to pay tribute to a television programme that has won all our hearts with its deft mixture of compassion, social concern, self-sufficiency,— the absolute imperative of standing on our own two feet, or stumps, as the case may be,—and not least that great rollicking good humour which is one of the shining merits of the British people: our ability to poke fun at ourselves and laugh at our own misfortunes.

"I refer, of course, to *Bootstraps*, which tonight is to be honoured with a special award for its outstanding contribution to current affairs entertainment.

"Its consummate triumph, I believe, is in demonstrating our very real concern for the more unfortunate members of society,—these wretched abnormalities you see displayed before you,—while at the same time administering a short sharp shock to the consciences, so-called, of the shirkers and spongers and backsliders, providing the timely reminder that no one gets a free

176

ride any more, and shaming them (if such creatures can be shamed) into hauling themselves out of the pit of sloth and sickening self-pity into making a genuine effort to contribute positively to society instead of being a dead weight and a drain on its resources.

"This brilliant concept was the brainchild of producer Bryce Ransom and his associate producer Mzzz Virgie Hance. Together they identified a need in mass televisual entertainment and set about filling that need with quite remarkable instinct, flair and professional skill. It is an object lesson to us all; the principle of freedom-loving competitive democracy in action, made flesh so to speak.

"I needn't add that such a programme would not find favour, much less receive the breath of life, in certain other regions of the globe it would be churlish to mention, except to remark in passing that one of them lies roughly above latitude 43 degrees north and covers 8,649,489 square miles, the eastern portion of which is snow-covered for much of the year.

"However, this isn't the moment to point the finger at non-democratic totalitarian slave states where the secret police rule the roost and pull you out of bed at two o'clock in the morning; rather we should rejoice in our own self-enlightenment, in our unflinching honesty and bravery in allowing this programme to be made and shown to a primetime mass audience. Where else in the world, we might legitimately ask ourselves, could this happen? I think we know the answer.

"Not least in this wonderful success story was the inspired choice as presenter of a man who rose from total obscurity to become a megamedia star in his own right. A true 'man of the people'. A man after my own heart.

"From humble beginnings, by dogged perseverance, unstinting application and the sweat of his brow, Jack Vail carved out a career for himself in the dynamic and highly competitive world of television. Not for him the moping miseries of the fainthearts and the whingeing fringers; no, here was a man determined to claw his way from the bottom of the social slag-heap come hell or high water.

177

"Without the benefits of a privileged background and university education, Jack Vail proved to one and all that upward mobility is no empty myth. Given the right kind of stuff, which he has in ample abundance, he showed how an ignorant and uncouth *swmbwl*, a onetime manual worker and ex-union member no less, can throw off the shackles of the underclass into which he was born, rejecting the spurious 'values' of apathy and morbid defeatism of that same class, and overcome all obstacles to emerge triumphant, a credit to himself and to society at large."

The stewards and security men were becoming desperate, as was the Cabinet Minister, or perhaps it was a Lord, who had planned the evening's itinerary with stopwatch precision. By this time the deformed imbeciles should have sung their song and been long gone from the bunker, whereas the PM's prolix and discursive peroration,—already overrunning its allotted span by several minutes,—had long exceeded their capacity to remain quietly seated, composed, and continent. Indeed, there was some doubt now as to whether they would even remember the words they had been taught parrot-fashion so painstakingly over recent weeks.

As if this weren't bad enough, the smell was making a number of people physically ill. Several had been supported or bodily carried to the rest rooms, while others had moved as far away from the dais as the confines of the hall would allow.

Rumblings of unrest and disgruntlement if not actual outrage were heard: whoever was responsible for staging this farce quite evidently couldn't organise a piss-up in a brewery.

"Therefore it is with great pride and pleasure" (visible signs and audible sighs of relief) "that I call upon Jack Vail to receive, on behalf of the entire production team, this award for *Bootstraps*, in recognition of outstanding contribution to the cultural lifeblood of this nation,—"

Vail buttons up his tuxedo, straightens his black tie, and starts forward.

"—a heritage which has coursed through the veins of Englishmen and women since the time of Shakespeare and even before. While we possess such riches we shall want for nothing. Let the hordes of barbarians come: they cannot withstand a nation united in blood and tradition, a nation that has scorned the slings and arrows of outrageous fortune and shrugged off the scourge of the swastika as even now it spits defiance at the godless philistines of the red star war machine."

Having skirted the sticky brown pool, Vail has paused uncertainly with one foot on the bottom step. People in the crowd are urging and shooing him on, frantic to get the bloody thing over and done with, though still Vail hesitates, waiting to be given the signal to proceed.

"It does the soul good to know that in these troubled times of ours, beset as we are by so many problems, there still beats in the heart of this great nation that indomitable spirit,—"

Vail cautiously slides his foot onto the next step but then pauses, suspended, halfway up and halfway down the short flight of steps. Voices urge him on. He receives a savage push in the small of the back, staggers forward, recovers, holds his ground.

"—which over the centuries has kept us whole, pure and inviolate, indifferent to the fickle sway of opposing ideological tyrannies which afflict much of this planet. Thank God that in such an uncertain ever-changing world we remain steadfast and firm, rooted like an aged oak in the nourishing loam of our native land. Let them try and shift us if they can and if they dare; as a great man once said: 'We will take some shifting!'."

Unaware, too weary and despondent to entertain the faint hope that the speech has ended, the audience is silent in the vast shuffling bunker with its curved roof and walls pimpled with condensation. Someone hisses at Vail, who breaks from his paralysed trance and stumbles the last few steps onto the dais.

As the trophy,—a replica of a rebuilt and refurbished Harrods in pristine bronze,—is presented to Vail, the deformed imbeciles break raggedly into the song of praise in honour of the PM, a moment for which they have waited with such patience and fortitude, their innocent little hearts overflowing with gratitude and joy,—gratitude and joy, it needs be said, they feel with total sincerity and yet haven't the slightest conception why they ought to feel these sentiments nor to whom they should be properly addressed.

No matter; it is enough for the television cameras that they are seen to express them.

Their song sounds to Vail like the wails and agonised bellows of a colony of sea-cows in labour. Added to the smell it is well-nigh intolerable, and there is a surreptitious yet steady stream of movement to the exits. Patriotism has its limits, Bomb or no Bomb.

Vail's party at the bar is flushed and all aglow with triumph and alcohol. Bryce Ransom's blue temples are throbbing fit to burst and Virgie Hance has five cigarettes going all at once, one for each orifice. Mrs Stretcher, one of Vail's keenest fans, is swollen with pride, bosom pounding madly and on the verge of orgasm, as if he were her own son.

In his pocket Ed Flesh fingers the touch-sensitive buttons on a slim stainless steel calculator, boosting percentages, carrying decimal points and adding noughts in a delirium of ecstasy, while Laine Vere Jumper is chin-wagging with an old chum from Balliol, the Honourable Guy Naecological, he hasn't clapped eyes on in a donkey's age.

Now with the moment to hand and destiny within his grasp Vail finds himself encumbered with the Harrods trophy, which is stupendously heavy, pulling his arms to the floor. The PM is smiling into his face, one hand raised in acknowledgement of the ragged wailing song, the applause and cheers from the body of the hall.

From the corner of his eye he sees an aide slip a familiar pink and black capsule into the PM's hand, which undercover of that same hand smothering a cough vanishes in a trice and is washed down with a sip of mineral water.

Vail still hasn't solved the problem of what to do with the trophy, whose weight is tearing his arms from their sockets. In desperation he looks over his shoulder for assistance and a burly security man steps forward and relieves him of his burden.

Vail's arms are numb and his funnybones are tingling, but at least his hands are free. He flexes his fingers experimentally.

The bunker shudders, dust sifts through cracks in the ceiling, the lighting blinks, dims, fails, goes out.

Blackness.

Feet stamp and slither over the deformed imbeciles in the headlong rush. The owners of the feet have no idea where they're rushing to; after all this is supposed to be the safest spot within Greater London.

[*Vail doesn't know, and is never to know, that the tremor felt in the bunker was caused by ten pounds of gelignite in the emergency generator room, placed there by Fully Olbin's terrorist cell, who have at last managed to do something right.*]

At that moment he doesn't care, has other things on his mind, his hands closed and locked round a warm throat.

Vail increases the pressure voluptuously, thinking of Mira and Bev and all the others. It won't bring them back and it probably won't alter or improve matters one jot, but it feels so good. His anger (an emotion!) gives him hands of iron.

He increases the pressure further, hardly noticing the feeble flailing of limbs underneath him. He can feel the corded muscles and ligatures in the neck swelling and writhing under his hands like a bundle of live snakes.

Vail keeps on increasing the pressure, squeezing tighter and tighter until his fingers interlock round the back of the neck and his thumbs sink up to the second joint in the slack flesh of the throat.

Vail keeps up the pressure, not relenting, not relinquishing his iron grip on the pipeline, now constricted and closed shut, tight, nary the eye of a needle's worth of squinting gap inside his crushing hands.

Years pass, decades, and his hold never breaks, never wearies. The limbs have ceased to flail, and Vail is kneeling on the chest of a dead lifeless weight, holding the throttled neck in both hands like a wrung chicken.

A pencil beam illuminates the black-lipped mask and staring bloodshot eyes in a coin of light and a voice murmurs in his ear: "That should be enough."

"Enough," Vail replies

with a smile,

"is never

enough."

They have to break his grip.

4TH SECTION   MOTORWAY (II)

In some respects it was similar to my sojourn in the United Dairies tanker except that I was crossing the wire in the opposite direction and the leaking liquidy cargo in which I wallowed up to my armpits consisted of embryonic humans heaped on top of one another in a squelchy mass: the victims of toxic poisoning and radioactive decay who had so recently wailed their cretinous dirge in the PM's honour being returned by military transport whence they came.

From the little I can remember all was darkness and confusion in the bunker, everyone running several different ways at once and slipping and sliding on the deformed imbeciles whose faint mewing cries of terror and muffled squeaks of pain were lost in the general mad scrambling panic.

I do know that I was roughly,—brutally you might say,— manhandled off the dais and tossed from hand to unseen hand like a rag doll. At the time I thought *This is it. This is where you get yours. It's the Tower for you m'lad.* Instead of which I was thrown headfirst into the type of large metal skip builders use to dispose of their rubbish and landed in a morass of small bodies with stubby extensors, some of which appeared to be lifeless although still warm and twitching.

The skip was then hoisted by hydraulic means between davits and locked fast and we set off, rocking and swaying, the contents sloshing to and fro, in the dead of night. Though it was cold, this being Decemberish, I was kept warm as toast by being immersed armpit-deep in the lumpy mire of human flesh and waste product.

It was a long journey. I dozed. The stars rocked overhead. One of the creatures nearby, whose rudimentary features I could just discern, started to sing. Other voices joined in. It was the song they had been taught by an official from the Ministry of DIs, the last song, indeed the very last words, to be heard by the PM.

> Thank you for the food we eat
> Thank you for the world so sweet
> Thank you for the birds that sing
> Thank you God for everything.

Towards dawn we were a fair distance up the M1, near to Watford Gap I guessed. It had to be a guess because I couldn't see over the side of the skip.

I was still puzzling over my predicament and how it was, under the circumstances, I had come to be in it. Why was I here and not in police custody? The voice murmuring in my ear, the one that said "That should be enough," hadn't belonged to Fully Olbin, Urban Brown or Tex Rivett; in fact, as I only now realised, it hadn't been an English voice at all, or Australian, but American,—

This was such an odd revelation that I mused over it until we came off the motorway at Leicester (it was now daylight and I could read the overhead signs) and were heading east on the A607. The PM was fervently, indeed passionately, pro-American, had even abdicated certain sovereign rights in order to appease them and curry political favour. I couldn't understand it. But then international diplomacy never has been my strong point.

We pulled off the main road and were thrown about quite a bit as the transporter jolted along a narrow rutted lane. Sparse black branches went by as we wound deeper and deeper into the countryside. From the odour of putrefaction I judged that quite a few of my companions had died in the night. Come to that, I wasn't feeling too clever myself.

We passed through some kind of chain-link fence dotted along the top with what I took to be festive balls of cotton wool but were in fact white ceramic insulators. The transporter stopped and I could hear men's voices. They sounded tired. Somebody cracked a joke but no one laughed.

It worried me that they might decide to glance over the side of the skip,—I had a brother-in-law who was a driver and I knew that they usually checked their loads after a long trip. There was nowhere to hide, and my difference, as an adult and whole person, would be spotted immediately. I could only pray that they didn't think it worthwhile checking a load of slops, added to which the smell was enough to deter anyone and would in itself be adequate confirmation that the cargo was still, in a manner of speaking, in one piece.

Having nothing better to do I let my head rest on something soft and looked at the sky. It was an unbroken blanket of grey, grim and wintry-looking, piles of dirty clouds tumbling along under a steady biting wind.

After a while the blunt rounded top of a dark-green storage silo caught my eye. It had one of those circular stairways going round and round the structure up to a gantry. On the silo itself were painted the faded yellow letters UCP in an ornate and old-fashioned script.

A secret base for the Under-Cover Police outside the wire? A detention camp where they interrogated dissidents and political undesirables? An elimination centre,—part of the U.M.P.S. Programme I had heard people talk about but had never been sure actually existed?

This speculation, somewhat futile and unproductive lacking further information, was terminated as with a great coughing roar the transporter's engine started up again. The skip swayed to and fro as we moved off, breaking the scum and sending a warm watery brownish wave lapping over my head. The taste on my lips was vile: I preferred bollock-freezing milk to this any day.

In a couple of minutes the vehicle stopped, there was a crunching of gears, a billowing of blue diesel fumes, and we reversed into a vast shed or warehouse with a corrugated asbestos roof high above. Chains rattled and the engine changed pitch to a shrill whine as the hydraulics took the strain, lifting the skip between the davits and lowering it to the ground. Doors slammed, the transporter moved off, we were left alone in silence.

Wading and treading through the mire, pushing lumps aside, I pulled myself over the side and dropped, dripping-wet, to the floor. At once I felt the cold strike through me and my teeth started chattering.

There appeared to be machinery in the darker recesses of the building. I could see metal ducting and pipes, levers and gauges and large dials with red needles. Evidently a processing plant of some description.

I also noticed that the skip was resting on a series of metal rollers, the type of conveyance system used in engineering works to move heavy loads about.

Even then it didn't dawn on me what all this paraphernalia was for; and I don't think it was stupidity on my part so much as plain ignorance. I was still trying to figure out what possible use the Under-Cover Police could have for a couple of tons of mushy DIs rapidly going off.

The plant must have been automated or at least operated by remote-control because there was no one about when the machinery started up and the skip began to move. It trundled along the rollers for about fifteen yards and was brought to a halt by a pair of buffers. The whole apparatus then tilted and the contents spilled into a concrete pit which extended deep below ground level. As they slopped over the rim I heard weak snatches of dreadful melody . . . *thank you for the world so sweet . . . thank you for the birds that sing* . . . as they slid down and were swallowed up in final darkness.

From beneath my feet came muffled churning and gurgling sounds. The floor trembled. Lights lit up on the gauges. Needles quivered and swung round the dials. Whatever the process was, it had started.

In another part of the building, beyond the panel of controls with the levers and winking lights, I found out what it was.

Bales of compressed glutinous cattle cake came tumbling down a metal chute onto a conveyor belt which carried them to a bay where they were picked up and stacked ten high by a mechanical grab. Stupid of me not to have realised before,—but the plain fact was that I had become accustomed to the new meaning of the acronym "UCP" and all but forgotten the old one. I should have known that beyond the wire ordinary people were still eating tripe and pigs' trotters.

It had been a miserable, gloomy, depressing day to begin with, and this being the 22nd December, the shortest day of the year, it was very nearly dark by three o'clock in the afternoon when I set off across the bare fields. Behind me the red light on top of the silo glowed like a ruby.

I felt almost happy, I think. At least I was outside the wire and I was free. I could return to the north and settle back into some sort of normality. If I grew a beard people might not even recognise me. Most likely I would sink back into my old drinking habits, hanging round my old haunts, fraternising with my old cronies. There didn't seem a lot else to do.

If I kept heading east, I thought, trudging across the fields in the darkness, I should strike the A1 in about an hour, just south of Grantham.